"Don't. Please Don't," She Whispered.

His lips brushed teasingly against her neck as he muttered, Don't what?"

"Don't *touch* me!"

"Ah, but I have to . . ." He smiled down lazily at her and his hands moved around to pull the pins from her chignon. Her hair tumbled down in golden disarray. "So this is the real Leigh! Too lovely to resist!"

"No!" She gasped, as she looked up at him with reproachful eyes.

His dark eyes narrowed. "All right, now that I have your undivided attention, suppose you tell me why you were so anxious to come here?" His tone changed abruptly, and a threatening note came into his voice. "Or is the answer obvious?"

DONNA VITEK

firmly believes that "I would probably never have learned to enjoy writing as much as I do" without the helpful influence of her husband, Richard. This is her second Silhouette Romance.

Dear Reader,

Silhouette Romances is an exciting new publishing series, dedicated to bringing you the very best in contemporary romantic fiction from the very finest writers. Our stories and our heroines will give you all you want from romantic fiction.

Also, *you* play an important part in our future plans for Silhouette Romances. We welcome any suggestions or comments on our books, which should be sent to the address below.

So enjoy this book and all the wonderful romances from Silhouette. They're for *you!*

Silhouette Books
Editorial Office
47 Bedford Square
LONDON
WC1B 3DP

DONNA VITEK

Showers of Sunlight

Published by Silhouette Books

For my father - Terry Kimel

First printing 1981

British Library C.I.P.

Vitek, Donna
Showers of sunlight. - (Silhouette romance)
I. Title
813'.54 (F)   PS3572.17/

ISBN 0-340-26736-4

Printed and bound in Canada for Hodder and Stoughton Paperbacks, a division of Hodder and Stoughton Ltd., Mill Road, Dunton Green, Sevenoaks, Kent (Editorial Office: 47 Bedford Square, London, WC1 3DP)

For my father—
Terry Kimel

Chapter One

"Could you explain to me how one saint is buried in three different churches?" Leigh Sheridan asked wryly. Her turquoise eyes sparkled with amusement as she walked down the cathedral's stone stairs. "Have you noticed that at each cathedral we've visited, the guide has told us in an awed whisper that we're standing before the tomb of St. Sebastian? I get the idea somebody's not being completely truthful, don't you?"

Walking beside her, Stefano Marvini stuffed his hands into his trouser pockets and stared ahead sullenly.

"I'm sorry to hear you doubt the honesty of my countrymen," he finally mumbled, a sulky frown marring his dark brow. "If you aren't enjoying seeing the sights, perhaps you should tell me what you *would* like to do the rest of the morning."

As she slowly counted to ten, Leigh flicked the thick long plait of shining honey-blond hair back over her shoulder.

"Did I say I wasn't enjoying the sightseeing?" she responded at last, her calm tone belying the impatience that was steadily rising in her. "I was only making a little joke, Stefano. I didn't mean to insult you and all Italy. Do you possibly think you can find it in your heart to forgive me?"

Though her tone was unmistakably teasing, he shrugged insolently, hunching his shoulders as his moody black eyes swept over her. Then, without warning, he caught both her hands in his, pressing them against his chest.

"Why are we wasting our time like a couple of silly tourists, anyway, *cara mia?*" he whispered urgently, lifting one small hand to his lips. "You look so beautiful in that little white sundress that I'd much rather be at home—alone with you—than out here trudging through cathedrals. Let's go back, hmmm? We could go for a swim in the pool."

As Leigh gently disentangled her hands she spied the perfect diversion over his left shoulder.

"Oh look, an ice cream shop. That would be delicious, don't you think? It's so warm in this sun. I think I'll have a lemon ice like I had the other day. What was it you called it? A *granita di* . . ."

"*Limone,*" Stefano said sullenly, guiding her across the narrow cobblestone street with obvious reluctance. After silently pulling out a chair for her at one of the small round terrace tables, he sat down across from her and glared at a young waitress until she hurried over.

"I thought you'd have something too, or I wouldn't have suggested we stop here," Leigh commented after the girl had gone away again. "Are you sure you don't want anything?"

"Nothing they serve here," he answered sharply, drumming his fingers on the tabletop. "Lemon ices are for children. I'd prefer a tall, strong drink."

"A little early in the day to start drinking, isn't it?"

The drumming of his fingers ceased as he looked her

over with brooding intensity. "You, my dear Leigh, would undoubtedly drive a saint to drink," he said at last, adjusting the lapels of the white silk shirt that was unbuttoned halfway down his chest. "It's quite obvious that you're avoiding being alone with me—and frankly, I'm baffled. What is this game you're playing? You accept my invitation to Rome and, when we arrive, you start playing—what is it you Americans say? Hard to get? Why are you playing hard to get with me?"

"Because I came here for a job, not a summer fling, and you know that, Stefano," she said tersely, her patience wearing very thin. "You told me your father had heard of a job with one of the news agencies here that would be just perfect for me. So why hasn't he said anything to me about it since I arrived? I'm beginning to wonder if you just told me all of that to get me to come with you. Did your father ever really say he'd found a position for me?"

"What a suspicious little girl you are, *cara mia,*" Stefano said, flashing her one of his most charming smiles. "I assure you my father can persuade one of his friends to hire you as a correspondent."

"No doubt he could if he knew that's why I came to Rome," Leigh responded coolly, no longer susceptible to his beguiling ploys. "But he doesn't know that, does he? Because you never talked to him about me before we got here, did you? He probably doesn't even know my real reason for being in Rome, does he?"

"Now, *cara,* don't—"

"Does he?" she repeated solemnly. "The truth, please."

"All right, all right, I haven't actually spoken to him about a job for you—yet," Stefano admitted, carelessly shrugging his shoulders. "But I will, I promise, so don't worry. At the moment, he is busy acquiring another newspaper in Milano. When that is accomplished in a week or so, I'll speak—"

"A week or so?" Leigh exclaimed softly. "But I can't

impose on your family that long—especially since they don't even know why I'm here. They already look at me like they don't quite approve of me, and I can't say I blame them. They must think I came to Rome with you just to have a high old time."

"And if you had come only for the fun of it, would that be so terrible?" Stefano countered glibly, while tapping the end of a Turkish cigarette against the tabletop. "You're much too serious, *cara mia.* A young woman of twenty-one shouldn't think of work during her first visit to Rome. This is a city made for love."

With a sigh of pure frustration, she turned aside in her chair and stared down at her hands clutching the white lace shawl she had worn to cover her bare shoulders in the cathedral. Her fingers began nervously plucking at the fine mesh as a knot of dismay tightened in her stomach. She should never have come here—not with Stefano. Now she could see what a mistake it had been. He had changed since their arrival two weeks ago; and the change was not to her liking. During the prior month in San Francisco, he had been a delightful companion. The heir to an Italian publishing empire, he had been observing the operational procedures of the newspaper where Leigh worked. Though she had been only the underling assigned to run any errands he might want done, he had treated her more like an equal. Actually, he had flirted outrageously with her and she had been flattered by his boyish Continental charm. Yet now, here in Rome, the boyishness was beginning to seem more like immaturity and the previous light flirtation began to take a ridiculously serious turn. Suddenly, he seemed intent on seducing her and his "Latin lover" act was beginning to grate on her nerves. Sometimes she suspected he had invited her here, hoping to flaunt her as his American conquest and now that she was failing to cooperate, his charm was fading as quickly as her patience.

Now the budget cut that had eliminated her position

on the newspaper staff in San Francisco seemed incredibly ill-timed. Losing her job had made her far too susceptible to Stefano's blithe promises. Obviously, she would have been wiser if she had heeded her parents' advice instead and gone home to Seattle until she could find another job in the States. Unfortunately, she had decided they were trying to be overprotective, as usual, and the desire to reassert her independence had influenced her to accept Stefano's invitation. But if the job he had promised failed to materialize, she would have to admit she should have listened to her parents' advice. Worse yet, she would even have to ask them to lend her the money for airfare home—and that would only strengthen their old-fashioned belief that she was too young and too inexperienced in the ways of the world to take care of herself. Since she was the baby of the family, they and her two older brothers had always incorrectly assumed that she needed a keeper. She wanted badly to prove them wrong. Somehow she had to persuade Stefano to make good his promises.

Thoughtfully tapping her forefinger against her lips, she observed him through the thick fringe of her dark brown lashes.

"Well, are you ever really going to talk to your father about a job for me?" she asked at last. "Or *did* you just invite me here for a summer fling?"

"*Amare mia,*" he whispered admonishingly, laying his hand over hers on the tabletop. "You do me an injustice, I assure you. Though I wouldn't object to spending every minute of this summer with you, I realize you want to become a correspondent with one of the news services. So I will make every effort to see that you do. I promise."

"But when, Stefano?" she persisted softly, easing her hand out from beneath his caressing fingers. "This sightseeing is lovely but I can't go on imposing on your parents indefinitely. I need to start working so I can get some experience covering real news stories. Lord knows, I didn't get any the two months I worked in San Francisco. Reporters right out of college get all the cat-up-a-tree-rescued-by-firemen stories."

Laughing, his good humor obviously restored, Stefano leaned back in his chair, allowing his admiring gaze to wander over her once again.

"You are such fun, *cara,*" he murmured. "Italian girls rarely speak their minds the way you do and, I must say, I find your independence very refreshing."

"You're avoiding the real issue again," Leigh reminded him, a no-nonsense gleam in her lovely aqua eyes. "Now, are you or are you not going to speak to your father? And if you are, when?"

"Soon, I promise."

"How about tonight?"

"Tonight? Oh, all right, if you insist, I shall speak to him tonight." Heaving a resigned sigh, Stefano glanced at his expensively thin gold wristwatch, then up again at Leigh with a hopeful smile. "Now that that's all settled, why don't we go back to the villa for a swim in the pool?"

"How about a swim at the beach instead?" Leigh suggested, remembering his hands tended to wander her way incessantly whenever she found herself alone with him. "You haven't forgotten, have you, that you promised to take me to the beach at Terracina? Today would be the perfect time to go."

"But the pool . . ."

"I'd really love to see the beach," Leigh insisted, nodding her thanks to the waitress who served the lemon ice. Then as the girl departed, Leigh smiled across the table. "Please? Why swim in a pool when we could be swimming in the beautiful Mediterranean?"

Faced with such logic, Stefano finally inclined his head in agreement. But later as they walked to the car, he abruptly drew her into the doorway of a small camera shop, pressed a light kiss on her lips, then pulled away to trace a fingertip over the slight beginning curve of her breasts above the bodice of her sundress. Before Leigh could protest, the shop door opened and a tall dark man in his thirties observed Stefano's caress, disdain in his icy green eyes. With a deep-throated "*Scusa,*" he compelled Stefano to move away, and, as the man stepped sideways between them, facing Leigh, her cheeks flamed as she bent her head, feeling rather than seeing the disapproving stare he gave her.

"Why must you embarrass me that way?" she asked Stefano irritably when the man was gone. "Did you see how he looked at me? Like I was some kind of . . ."

"Why do you care?" Stefano asked with an infuriating shrug. "It does not matter what a stranger thinks of you."

"It matters to me, so for goodness' sake, stop attacking me—especially in public!" Taking a calming breath she added, "Oh, come on, let's go to the beach. Okay?"

"Okay," Stefano agreed. But judging by the sullen look on his face, he was far from pleased.

During the afternoon at Terracina, however, Leigh's enthusiastic enjoyment of the soft, warm Mediterranean waters began to lighten his mood. By the time they left for his villa, he was acting more like the Stefano she had known in San Francisco, so she was feeling very optimistic when she excused herself immediately after dinner to give him the chance to speak to his father as he had promised. Surely Stefano at his most charming couldn't fail to get what he wanted, even from an obvious workaholic like Umberto Marvini, who usually closeted himself in his study every evening with his briefcase for company. Super-businessman that he was, though, he still doted on his only son. Leigh was fairly confident that any reasonable request Stefano made would be granted. Besides, she wasn't asking for something for nothing. She planned to work very hard if given the opportunity to prove herself as a reporter.

To take her mind off Stefano's mission, as she ascended the curving marble stairs to her room she allowed herself to bask in the luxurious atmosphere of the villa. She had never seen a home as magnificent as this one. It still astounded her that she was actually an invited guest at one of the most prestigious estates on the picturesque Appian Way. Up on the second-floor gallery, she looked back down at the grand hall she had just left, finding a true, simple beauty in the mosaic-tiled floor and the clean lines of the slender fluted columns that supported the domed ceiling. The entire villa presented the same uniformly elegant image, yet, even set amid umbrella pines and neat cypress trees and surrounded by formal lawn and gardens, there seemed to be something lacking—perhaps a certain warmth. Like many stately mansions it sometimes seemed more a museum, and as Leigh walked toward the west wing she couldn't help thinking in clichés: the villa was a nice place to visit but she wouldn't care to live here indefinitely.

Leigh's own room seemed almost sinfully opulent. As she went inside she looked around with renewed wonder at the ivory-inlaid furniture, the richly woven rugs on gleaming hardwood floor, and the carved arched doors that led to the luxuriously appointed adjoining bath. Accustomed to far more plebeian surroundings, she could hardly understand how Stefano could take such extravagance for granted. Of course, there were drawbacks to being wealthy in Italy these days. Kidnapping for ransom was rampant and the Marvini estate was guarded day and night by a small army of men. Whenever Stefano left the grounds, a rather morose, hulking bodyguard was never far behind. To Leigh, it seemed a pretty sad, unfree way to live and she found that, despite all their material wealth, she didn't envy the Marvini family at all.

Sitting down before a marble-topped vanity, she began brushing the long silky strands of her gleaming hair, still trying not to wonder how Stefano was progressing with his father. So it was something of a relief when her thoughts were diverted by a soft tapping on her door. Turning on the velvet-cushioned vanity scat, she smiled as Signora Marvini glided gracefully into the room.

Stefano's mother was a pleasant person and very lovely with fine patrician facial features. Despite her rather quiet, remote personality, she had always been quite kind to Leigh. Tonight was no different. Unnecessarily smoothing the sleek dark hair that coiled into a chignon at the nape of her slender neck, Signora Marvini smiled back and poised herself prettily on the edge of a tapestry-upholstered chaise longue.

"I wanted to assure myself that you are not upset because your visit with us must be abbreviated," she began abruptly, her stilted English somehow adding more mystery to an already confusing statement, as she lifted her hand in a vague gesture of apology. "Of course, I'm sure my son explained to you that we must ask you to leave only because his Zia Lucia and three of her spinster daughters have been planning for months to come stay the entire summer with us. And, unfortunately, Lucia is a very old-fashioned woman. Innocent as it is for you to visit Stefano in our home, she would be shocked to find you here without a chaperon. I wish you to know that I regret this inconvenient disruption in your *vacanza*—how do you call it?—your holiday. But you do understand my position, *si?*"

"Si, signora," Leigh murmured automatically, though it took a few seconds for the pieces of the puzzle to fall together in her befuddled mind. When she fully realized she was being asked to leave the villa, her first

reaction was an incongruous desire to laugh aloud as she wondered just how Stefano had meant to get out of this predicament. He really was the most irresponsible rogue she had ever met; at the very least, he could have told her she would have to leave, as his mother had apparently expected him to do. Yet, he hadn't. Leigh decided she might as well pretend he had, if only to save Signora Marvini embarrassment. Smiling, she nodded. "I understand perfectly, *signora*—I have some very old-fashioned relatives too. Besides, you've already been very kind to me the past two weeks. I want to thank you for inviting me to stay here. You have a beautiful home and I've really enjoyed my visit."

"The pleasure has been ours, I assure you," Stefano's mother said softly as she got up to walk toward the door. "Well, now I will leave you to get ready because I am certain my son plans to take you out tonight."

Leigh glanced at the delicate enamelled clock on the vanity, and was surprised to see that it was already past ten-thirty. Having dinner fashionably at nine o'clock didn't leave much time for a nightlife.

"I don't know if we'll go out or not, late as it is," she told the older woman. "I guess it depends on how long Stefano talks to his father."

"Oh, but they have finished their little chat," Signora Marvini informed her. "Actually my husband was called back to his office soon after dinner, so I would think Stefano still has plans for the evening."

"Oh, he always has lots of plans," Leigh muttered to herself after his mother had said goodnight and left. Unfortunately, none of those plans seemed to work out quite the way he said they would. In all fairness, Leigh couldn't blame him completely for the mess she was in. He hadn't dragged her here to Rome; she had simply decided to come without giving the matter enough thought. Now she had no choice except to admit that to herself. Even if Signor Marvini did miraculously provide a job for her, she would be hard pressed to live on the little bit of money she had until her first paycheck. "Nincompoop," she called herself, wrinkling her nose at her reflection in the gold-framed mirror. Sighing, she stood and smoothed the skirt of her midnight blue jersey dress; her hands ceased moving abruptly when she heard a soft persistent scratching on her door.

It was Stefano. When Leigh turned the knob to release the catch, he moved swiftly into the room, glancing back over his shoulder as if he didn't want to be seen by anyone in the hall.

"Most of the servants still live in the Dark Ages," he whispered dramatically. "They would be horrified if they saw me coming into your bedroom."

Rather irritated by his theatrics, Leigh waved a dismissive hand.

"Why didn't you tell me my staying here would inconvenience your mother?" she asked bluntly, tucking a strand of hair back behind her ear. "Really, Stefano, you're impossible. Frankly, I'm surprised you didn't just bring me here without even warning her, but. . . ." Leigh's words trailed off to silence as a flush darkened his cheeks beneath his tan. When he averted his eyes guiltily, she groaned. "Oh no, you *didn't* warn her, did you? You just brought me here and dumped me in her lap? And you told me she had offered to send me a written invitation!"

"But *cara,* I knew she wouldn't mind at all if I brought you home with me," he protested urgently, reaching for her hand then sighing when she pushed his away. "Truly, *amare mia,* she would have sent you a written invitation if I had asked her to. I—I just never got around to doing it."

"How dare you put me in such an awkward position?" Leigh asked heatedly, her blue eyes flashing. "Your parents must think I have no manners at all coming here without an invitation!"

"But that's not true. They both are enjoying your visit with us."

"That's not the point and you know it isn't!" With a flounce of her skirt, Leigh turned and marched to the window where she stared out at the dark shadows of the umbrella pines that bordered the sweeping lawn below. Taking a deep breath, she sought to control her irritation and after a moment she did manage to continue more calmly: "I think the best thing for me to do under these circumstances is to go home. Tomorrow, I'll wire my father and ask him to send me enough money to cover my airfare."

"No, you cannot do that!" Stefano protested vehemently, going to lay his hands tentatively on her shoulders. Murmuring her name, he turned her around to face him. "Please *cara mia,* stay so we can get to know each other better. Please, hmm?"

Leigh lifted her eyes heavenward with an exasperated sigh.

"If you want me to stay because you hope we'll become lovers, then you're wasting your time, Stefano," she told him frankly and without apology. "I didn't come here to get involved in an intimate relationship and I wish you'd stop assuming that I did."

"But why shouldn't I assume that?" he asked bewilderedly. "After all, you're one of those liberated American girls, aren't you?"

"Oh, for heaven's sake," she whispered incredulously, fighting a nearly overwhelming desire to laugh. "Don't tell me you're one of those men who believes a girl who acts like she can take care of herself must naturally be sexually active too? If you do believe that, then you're wrong. Being independent doesn't mean a girl is also promiscuous—not by a long shot. And I'm not interested in that kind of relationship right now—with you or with anybody else."

His surprised expression was almost comical as he muttered: "But I—I thought—"

"You thought wrong then," she interrupted wearily, escaping the hands that gripped her shoulders. Stepping away from him, she shook her head and gave him a rueful little smile. "We certainly got our signals crossed, didn't we? That's why I think it would be best if I just go back home."

"But I don't want you to go," he persisted, his tone rather childishly fervent. "And besides, don't you still want a job with one of the news services? I decided not to speak to my father tonight because—well, to be honest, he's a bit displeased with me lately; he thinks I've been spending far too much money. But when I do think it's safe to ask him a favor, I'm sure he'll be happy to help you. And until then, I'm sure I could persuade my mother to let you stay on here."

"Oh no, you won't either!" Leigh said emphatically. "I wouldn't dream of staying now—especially knowing she never invited me in the first place! I won't have her thinking I'm *completely* lacking in consideration."

"Then we could get you a place to stay in Rome instead," he suggested eagerly, never one to give up without an argument. "Then while we wait until I can talk to my father, we could still be seeing each other. How does that idea sound?"

"Very impractical since I have very little money, certainly not enough to rent a hotel room for more than a few days."

"But we could find you something less expensive," he insisted, nodding enthusiastically as if he believed that might help persuade her. "There are some very nice boarding houses. I could help you pay your rent."

"That's very kind, but no, thank you," she said hastily, wondering if he might consider her his mistress if he paid her rent. He *did* tend to look at life very immaturely. Turning away, she added: "I'd better just go home. That's really about the only thing I can do."

"No, it isn't, *cara;* you could get some other kind of employment!" he declared excitedly, catching her arm as she started to walk away. He laughed gleefully at his sudden inspiration. "Now, why didn't I think about that before? If you won't take money from me, then you could get another job until I talk to my father. And isn't it lucky? I happen to know a young lady who works in one of those employment agencies."

"Well, I don't know. I . . ."

"Admit it, *cara mia,*" he said rather smugly. "You don't want to go home after only two weeks here, not after your family advised you not to come."

He was right about that. Leigh had no desire to go back and face all those silent we-told-you-so looks. If only she could find some kind of temporary job here until Signor Marvini could help her get a position with one of the news services. . . . Tilting her head to one side, she eyed Stefano rather suspiciously, not at all sure she should trust him again.

"What kind of job?" she finally asked. "Do you really think I might find something that would pay me enough to rent a room somewhere?"

"But of course," he responded confidently, a victorious grin curving his lips. "So you will not think about going home again until I have talked to the young lady I know tomorrow, all right, *cara?*"

"Oh all right, I suppose I can wait until tomorrow," Leigh agreed at last. But she couldn't seem to muster much enthusiasm. Knowing Stefano as she did now, she feared he would find some way to botch up this plan too.

Amazingly, Stefano returned to the villa with reasonably good news late the next morning. Long before Leigh actually saw him in the formal rose garden, she heard his brisk footfalls resounding on the gleaming flagstone walkway. When he finally came into the arbor where she waited on a bench in the cool shade, she smiled hopefully and received one of his smuggest grins in response as he sat down beside her.

"I have found the perfect position for you, *cara mia,*" he said proudly, as if he were announcing the discovery of a new miracle drug. "It's temporary and the salary is fairly good. But best of all, you'll be close enough to Rome for me to see you on your day off every week."

Stilling the hand that began to slide around her waist, Leigh smiled wryly.

"Maybe you should tell me something about this job before we start making plans for my days off. What will I be doing? And where will I be doing it, if not in Rome?"

"I know you'll like it, *amare mia,*" Stefano said confidently, draping his arm across her shoulders. "Anybody would like the idea of living on the beautiful isle of Capri."

"Capri? But what—"

"You'll soon be a companion to a thirteen-year-old girl. Not a bad job, eh, as far as jobs go?"

"No, I guess it isn't," Leigh admitted, but she was frowning perplexedly. "Except I have no idea what the duties would be. What exactly does a companion to a thirteen-year-old girl do?"

"Keep her company, of course, and see that she's not lonely."

"But why should she be lonely in the first place?" Leigh persisted. "Doesn't she have any family? Who does she live with?"

"Does it matter?"

"Well, of course it matters. I'd like to know something about this girl before I agree to go live with her."

"All I can tell you is what my friend, Maria, told me. The girl lives with her uncle on Capri but he is a very busy man so she needs a companion." Stefano shrugged carelessly, as if he understood the situation completely. Reaching out, he drew Leigh into his arms and brushed his lips across her smooth ivory cheek as he whispered huskily, "And that's all you really need to know, isn't it, until you go to Capri on Friday? It is simply a job. I told you I would find something for you, didn't I? Perhaps now, you should prove you're no longer upset with me, hmm, *amare mia?*"

"Perhaps," Leigh agreed abstractedly, even as she pushed his hands away and moved beyond his reach. She hardly noticed the petulant frown that darkened his face as a result of her rejection. She was far too busy wondering why a girl of thirteen needed a paid companion. Even if her uncle was too busy to care about her, she should at least have friends to keep her from being too lonely. Yet obviously she didn't. Suddenly this little girl and her indifferent uncle became an intriguing mystery. And Leigh had never been able to resist a mystery.

Chapter Two

"There is only one thing Maria forgot to mention Wednesday," Stefano remarked casually as he careened his engine-red Ferrari around a hairpin curve on the scenic Amalfi Drive. "She called to tell me yesterday. It shouldn't be any real problem. Just a small one, really."

"Problem?" Leigh questioned, dragging her bemused gaze from the village of Positano that sloped steeply down the mountainside to the sea. A sudden sinking sensation dragged at her stomach at Stefano's words. She couldn't imagine what could possibly have gone wrong now. She did know that when he was involved, problems were very rarely small. Taking a deep breath, hoping to ease the knot of apprehension in her stomach, she eyed him suspiciously. "What kind of a problem are you talking about? I thought you'd told me everything you knew about this job."

"Oh, I did, honestly, *cara mia,* I did tell you everything," he assured her hastily, glancing at her for an instant before turning his attention back to the tortuously twisting road. "It was Maria who forgot to mention it to me."

"Forgot to mention what? What is the problem?"

"Well, it seems that this Signora Rossetti who is the housekeeper at the villa on Capri did specify what they wanted in a companion."

"Yes, you said they wanted a young Englishwoman or an American—so what's the problem? I qualify. I'm young and I'm an American."

"But you may be just a little *too* young," Stefano explained vaguely as he shifted uncomfortably in his seat. "You see, Maria realized yesterday that Signora Rossetti actually requested a woman in her late thirties or early forties."

"You must be kidding!" Leigh said disgustedly, raking her fingers through her silky windswept hair. She pressed her lips firmly together and counted to ten mentally again, as she had done almost habitually since she had arrived in Italy. She should have known Stefano would create another fiasco. He was the most irresponsible, disorganized human being she had ever met. She could hardly believe he was actually twenty-five years old. He acted more like an addle-brained teenager; she ached to tell him so. Instead, she managed to calm herself enough to mutter through clenched teeth: "Then if I don't qualify for this job, could you please tell me why we're on our way to Sorrento so that I can catch a boat to Capri? I should be in Rome, wiring my parents for airfare home. So if you would drive me back there immediately, I'd be eternally grateful."

"Now, *cara,* don't get all upset with me," he said cajolingly, shaking his head as she glared at him. "You're still going to have your job on Capri. If they want someone older, you will simply have to pretend you are older, that's all."

"Now how am I supposed to do that?" Leigh asked,

totally exasperated. "I can hardly convince people that I'm twenty-one! In case you haven't noticed, I have one of those silly little girl faces."

"You have a very lovely face," Stefano murmured, his eyes sweeping over her briefly. "But you are right. You do look very young. But if we could de-emphasize those big blue eyes and hide that glorious hair and conceal that very nice figure, I believe we could make you look old enough to satisfy Signora Rossetti. Surely she won't protest if you seem only a few years younger than she wants the girl's companion to be."

"I have no idea what you're talking about," Leigh responded stiffly. "And I'm not sure I want you to tell me. Even if I wanted to try to make myself look older, which I don't, it wouldn't work."

"Oh but it would," Stefano said confidently, veering the Ferrari onto the next wide shoulder off the road. Smiling, he reached behind the seats and extracted several boxes. "And I brought you here early so that you would have time to get into this little disguise."

Leigh stared bewilderedly at a sturdy pair of unattractive black oxford shoes, and three voluminous, drab caftans with long sleeves. When she saw the short brown wig in the box he opened, she began shaking her head emphatically.

"Oh no, if you expect me to dress up in that garb, you're crazy," she whispered incredulously. "Why, those shoes look like gunboats and those dresses, they're . . . they're just awful! And that wig! Good heavens, that thing on my head would drive me batty. Oh no, I wouldn't walk around in that get-up for anything in the world!"

Stefano's smile faded.

"I thought you wanted this job, Leigh. Remember, you don't want to go home yet. If you could just keep this job on Capri for a few weeks until I can talk to my father . . ."

"But I can't imagine wearing those shoes and dresses

and that wig for a few weeks, Stefano! Even if they weren't so hideous, they look unbearably hot—I get claustrophobia just looking at them."

"I don't see that you have any other choice," Stefano said bluntly. "Not if you refuse to take money from me. Unless, of course, you would rather wire your parents. Would you?"

"Well no, but—"

Finally they compromised. After a light lunch in a restaurant in Sorrento, Leigh went into the restroom to change her clothes. Five minutes later she stood in front of the small mirror in the ladies' lounge. Though it only gave her reflection from the waist up, that was enough to make her shudder. The voluminous navy blue dress, though obviously expensive, made her look like a fat crow. The stiff gabardine certainly concealed the slender yet curvaceous figure underneath. Even her shapely arms were covered by hot, long sleeves. The dress hung to just below her knees; completing the frumpy picture were the ridiculous heavy black oxfords which made her feel as if she had dipped her feet in cement and allowed it to harden.

She had refused to wear the wig, stuffing it into the wastepaper basket. Instead she pulled her honey-blond hair back severely from her face and twisted it into a tight knot at the nape of her neck. Then she perched the overly large tortoise-framed glasses Stefano had provided on her small straight nose. They were for show only; the lenses were clear glass but their shape didn't suit her and suddenly, in the dress, the shoes, and the glasses she looked the personification of tacky.

"Oh God, you're some beauty," she muttered to herself as she folded the ice-blue sundress and jacket she had been wearing and put them into the dress box with the remaining two dreary monstrosities.

A few minutes later, when she forced herself to join Stefano on the terrace of the restaurant, she noticed he no longer seemed eager to touch her. In fact, he moved several feet away from her as they stood at the railing, staring down at the bay of Naples. Glancing at him out of the corner of her eye, Leigh felt a nearly overwhelming urge to stamp the heel of one of her heavy clunky oxfords down hard on the soft leather toe of his Gucci loafer. Instead, she lifted her chin and gazed out across the crystal blue water of the bay at Naples shimmering in the early afternoon sun. Beyond, to the right, the still active Vesuvius, with a thin wisp of smoke from its peak, threatened the ruins of Pompeii. She sighed, her eyes drawn reluctantly away from the bay to the mountainous isle of Capri. When Stefano suggested they leave for the harbor below, she preceded him with mounting dread.

On the dock at Piccolo Sant' Angelo, they stood without talking until a group of noisy tourists began boarding the launch to Capri. Then, with a seriously mischievous gleam in her blue eyes, Leigh leaned close to Stefano and whispered: "Don't you want to kiss me goodbye?"

"Of course, *cara mia,*" he lied, brushing his lips hastily across her cheek.

"I hope you know I'll never forgive you for this," she said softly. "I never wanted to go to a lovely place like Capri, looking like my own great-grandma." Turning on her heel, she walked across the dock to board the boat without even acknowledging his assurances that he would be in touch with her soon. In a moment, as the boat swung out toward the open sea, she stood on deck gripping the railing, glaring back toward the dock where Stefano stood watching, his hands thrust into his pockets, a glum, yet somehow relieved, expression on his face.

She could have throttled him in that moment and thoroughly enjoyed doing it. He had a lot of nerve getting her into this ridiculous situation and then daring to show he was ashamed to be seen with her because of her awful clothes. She felt like such a fool. Luckily, however, no one seemed to be paying her the least bit of attention. Even the normally flirtatious Italian crewmen weren't giving her any second glances.

What a rotten way to begin a stay in Capri, she thought bleakly, staring ahead at the steeply sloped island rising out of the blue sea. If the people employing her could afford to live in a villa on a resort isle, they were undoubtedly members of the fashionably elite set. But she would have to walk around for the next few weeks, looking like the winner in a worst-dressed-woman-of-the-century contest. It simply didn't seem fair. She had never imagined she would spend her time in Italy participating in a ridiculous charade.

"Ah well, it can't last forever," she said softly, then forced herself to concentrate on the fresh sea breeze that was cooling her flushed cheeks. Capri loomed before the boat, its limestone cliffs gleaming in the showering sunlight. Leigh gazed up at its towering peaks, wondering where Villa Bianco was located.

As the boat docked at Marina Grande and Leigh disembarked, she detected the sweet enticing fragrance of innumerable flowers. As she hoisted her suitcase and totebag onto a bench on the quay, she had almost forgotten she was dressed like somebody's homeless old aunt. Before she could sit down, a gnarled old man approached, clutching a well-worn black beret in his hands. His brown face was lined with a network of wrinkles from years of exposure to wind and sun but his smile was welcoming—and a joy for Leigh to see, despite his two missing front teeth.

"Signorina Sheridan?" he inquired politely. When she nodded, he lifted her luggage, tossing his head to one side, indicating that she should follow. After settling her in the back of his fresh air taxi, he hopped in behind the steering wheel and gave her a grin over his shoulder before driving away from the harbor.

Though Leigh's Italian was very limited and the driver spoke little English, he kept up a constant chatter as they drove through the outskirts of the small town of Capri, where whitewashed buildings covered a gentle slope with cliffs rising on each side. As the taxi ascended the typically narrow, twisting road up Monte Tiberio, passing terraced vineyards, sloping fields of corn, and meadows dotted with olive, fig, and carob trees, the knot in her stomach tightened painfully. What if this ridiculous disguise failed to fool Signora Rossetti? It it didn't, would she even get a chance to prove herself a capable companion to a girl of thirteen? Her heart began to beat faster as the driver rounded a sharp curve in the road and turned off onto a stony private drive.

The white villa shimmered in the sunlight in a setting of lush green grounds dotted with carob and myrtle trees. Leigh breathed in the fresh fragrance of the small orange grove located on the south side of the house. With extreme reluctance she left the taxi and followed the driver as he carried her luggage along a pergola-shaded walkway to the massive arched front doors of the villa. Unaccustomed to the glasses perched on her nose, she fiddled with them nervously and shifted her feet as the man tapped the hammer of the gleaming brass door knocker.

A round little woman with greying black hair answered the knock, beaming a smile at the driver before giving a more cautious welcoming smile to Leigh. Then after rattling off Italian in a rapid staccato, she dug into a pocket of her voluminous black apron for money to pay for the taxi. After the man went happily on his way, she lifted Leigh's suitcase.

"You are late, *signorina,*" she announced unceremoniously, leading the way into a long, cool gallery with marble floors and a high arched ceiling. "We expected you this morning. Come along and I will show you your room. Then Signor Cavalli wishes to speak to you. He is displeased that you did not arrive this morning as arranged."

"I didn't realize I was late," Leigh said softly. "I was told I was expected this afternoon." Stefano had told her that. Of course anything he said was suspect and she supposed it was her own fault for not making certain he had his facts straight. She had enough working against her without incurring the displeasure of her new employer on the very first day.

As Leigh followed Signora Rossetti up a wide curving staircase to the long second-floor hall, however, she realized she had apparently passed the first hurdle. At least the housekeeper had let her in—so perhaps this outlandish garb she was wearing did make her look older after all, and not merely ridiculous. She certainly hoped it did—there should be some compensation for enduring these clodhopper shoes and this stifling hot dress.

"Here we are, signorina," Signora Rossetti said, stopping near the end of the hall to open a black arched door. "I hope you will be comfortable here."

Leigh stepped inside the large airy room and felt immediately cooler, due perhaps to the clean, uncluttered lines of the heavy furniture and to the fresh aqua color of the sheer drapes that billowed prettily in the breeze that blew gently through three wide windows. A counterpane of the same color covered the bed, which had an intricately carved headboard. It was a lovely, simple room and she preferred it over the too opulent room she had stayed in at Stefano's parents' villa. Actually, she preferred this entire, though smaller, estate to that other, much grander, one. No locked gates and fences protected a too obvious affluence here. No guards roamed the grounds, making the villa seem more like a prison. Laying her totebag on the carved wooden chest at the end of the bed, Leigh gazed at the frescoed panels of the wall, which depicted soothing pastoral scenes. She wriggled her hot toes inside her shoes. If only she could kick them off and remove the tent she was wearing for just a little while.

But the housekeeper was hovering by the door, as if waiting to lead her back downstairs.

"If you do not wish to freshen up, *signorina,* then we should go," Signora Rossetti prompted, as if on cue. "Signor Cavalli does not like to be kept waiting."

Smoothing back from her temple a wayward tendril of hair, Leigh nodded, then followed the woman back downstairs to the main gallery and along toward the back of the villa, where they stopped before a wide, carved door.

"There is only one strict rule in this house, *signorina,*" the housekeeper declared, pausing, her hand on the door knob. "But it is one you must never forget. You are not to discuss with anyone the personal lives of the *signor* and his niece. He is a man who likes privacy and he will not tolerate employees who gossip. You understand that?"

"Perfectly," Leigh murmured, feeling as if she had just been sworn in as an agent for the CIA. "I've never been much of a gossip, *signora,* so you don't have to worry about me."

"*Buono.*" Tapping once on the door, the woman turned the knob and indicated with a gesture that Leigh should step into the study. "The *signor* is in his darkroom," she explained. "You see that door with the red light shining above it? Do not open that door, *signorina.* Sit and wait until Signor Cavalli comes out."

Before Leigh could say anything, the study door was pulled close, but she hardly noticed anyway. *Cavalli.* She had thought she had heard that name before and the mention of the darkroom had triggered the memory. He was a young nature-photographer who occasionally, and brilliantly, turned his camera toward people as they were going about their normal everyday activities. Leigh had seen his collections and somehow he managed to capture something unique and very precious in each individual. He made photography an art and now she was more interested in meeting him. She knew little about his personal life. Last year her roommate, Linda, had swooned over a picture of him with a Hollywood starlet that she found in a celebrity magazine, but Leigh hadn't bothered to look at it. Linda swooned frequently over men—and often for no good reason.

Heeding Signora Rossetti's advice, Leigh sat down on the edge of a stuffed brown leather sofa and looked around the study curiously. Bookcases lined two of the walls from floor to ceiling, and except for the sofa, two matching chairs, and a desk covered with stacks of papers, there were no other furnishings in the room. It seemed like a nice, quiet place to be, but she was too nervous to benefit from the calming atmosphere. Clasping her shaky hands round her knees, she sighed dejectedly. She could have used the little bit of confidence that being dressed decently would have given her. In this ill-fitting, unflattering get-up, it was going to be doubly difficult meeting a man who was already impatient with her for being late. Would he be the moody artistic type who had little tolerance for the failings of mere mortals?

Even as she wondered about him, the red light went off and the door beneath it opened simultaneously. Jumping to her feet, Leigh automatically smoothed the folds of the navy blue horror she was wearing, and her cheeks burned with embarrassment as Marcus Cavalli stopped dead in his tracks, staring at her. Then her breath caught with the sudden realization that he was the man who had left the camera shop in Rome, the man who had stared at her so insultingly because Stefano's hands had been wandering over her. In that moment, she was actually glad she was disguised. He couldn't possibly recognize her in this garb. He was only staring because she looked so outrageously tacky.

Wishing she could sink right through the floor, she bent her head momentarily. Why hadn't she looked at the picture Linda had swooned over last year? If she had, she would have known what to expect and been more prepared for this. For once her roommate had been completely justified in oohing and ahing about a man. He wasn't handsome in the purely classical sense, he was undeniably attractive and more disturbingly masculine than any man Leigh had ever seen before. Tall and muscularly lean, he had thick, dark brown hair and strong, almost rugged, facial features. But it was his eyes that made her look up again. They were the clearest, deepest green she had ever seen—fringed with thick black lashes; she was mortified that they were observing her as if she might be a creature from outer space. She knew all too well that she looked as if she were auditioning for the part of the wicked witch in *The Wizard of Oz*.

At last, he regained his wits enough to walk across the room to his desk, but his eyes never left her as he sat down. "Miss Sheridan, I presume," he said, his voice low, pleasantly modulated, and completely lacking an accent.

"Why, you're American!" she observed compulsively. "I thought—well, the name Cavalli—I mean, I assumed—"

"I'm Italian-American, Miss Sheridan, born in Baltimore," he explained, a hint of amusement in his voice. "My parents weren't exactly fans of Benito Mussolini so they emigrated before the war and then liked the States so much that they stayed on." Leaning back in his swivel chair, he stroked the strong line of his jaw with one finger. "Now that you know some of my background, perhaps you'll sit back down and tell me about yourself. You can begin by explaining why you arrived late today."

Sinking back down on the sofa obediently, she murmured, "A mix-up about the time, I suppose. I understood I was expected some time this afternoon. I'm sorry if I caused anyone any inconvenience."

"No real harm done," he remarked graciously, his eyes sweeping over her and still retaining some of their former amazement. "Now, tell me what makes you feel you're qualified to deal with a thirteen-year-old girl? I've forgotten what the girl at the agency told me—how many years is it that you've taught school?"

Leigh nearly fainted. Her entire body burned for an instant, then went icy-cold as she stared at him. That idiot Stefano had done it to her again! He had actually told the agency that she had years of teaching experience because that had obviously been a requirement for the job. Now, she had no earthly idea of what to say or do.

"Well, I—actually, I—" she stammered then began again. "I mean, I—"

"More than five years?" he questioned. When she nodded automatically, he nodded also. "Fine. You've handled children with problems before then, I'm sure. That will come in handy because I'm sorry to say my niece, Angelica, can be very difficult sometimes. Frankly, I don't know her very well. Until her mother left her in my care for the summer, I rarely saw her—and never for very long. She is my younger brother's child, and since he and his wife are separated, Angelica and I never had many opportunities to get acquainted. She can be a very sweet child sometimes, though, and I brought you here because she is lonely."

"Oh, how sad," Leigh murmured, genuinely concerned. "Well, I only hope she'll enjoy my company. When may I meet her?"

"In a moment. First, I must explain to you about her paralysis."

"Paralysis?" Leigh exclaimed softly, horrified that Stefano had conveniently left out a detail as important as this. Then she recovered sufficiently to mask her shock. "I mean, I knew she wasn't well but—"

"She is confined to a wheelchair and has been for a year, Miss Sheridan. A victim of hysterical paralysis."

"You mean she—she should be able to walk but just can't?"

"Exactly. She thinks she can't, therefore she doesn't," Marcus said grimly. "She needs delicate handling, yet she must not be pampered unduly. She needs someone strong who won't cater to her every whim. Do you think you could be that kind of person, or would you let pity for her overwhelm common sense?"

"I think I'm a fairly sensible person, Signor Cavalli," Leigh responded rather defensively. "I don't usually let people walk over me, and I realize it wouldn't be good for Angelica to give her the idea that she can treat people as her servants simply because she can't walk."

"Good, we understand each other," he said, getting lithely to his feet. "I'll take you to meet her now. She's out on the piazza."

Leigh stood also, trying not to notice how the taut muscles of his thighs and shoulders strained against the sand-colored fabric of his trousers and shirt. When her eyes met the clear green of his again, and she saw that he was examining her curiously, she felt that burning heat in her cheeks again.

"How old are you, Miss Sheridan?" he asked abruptly, unaware that his question nearly sent her into cardiac arrest. "I'm merely curious. Of course, if you'd rather not tell me . . ."

"I'd rather not," she said hastily, forcing a horribly unconvincing little laugh. Averting her eyes, she stepped to the door with him. "You know, women don't like to divulge their ages."

"Whatever you say, Miss Sheridan," he said wryly, walking beside her down the hall.

As they walked across a handsomely furnished sitting room to the open French doors at the other end, Leigh couldn't help thinking how nice he was and how much she wished she didn't look like something the cat had dragged in. When he touched light fingers to her shoulder to indicate she should precede him out onto the piazza, she tried to ignore her own involuntary physical response, but it wasn't easy with him towering so close by, with the enticing warmth of his body exuding the spicy male fragrance of his after shave. Yet her attention was diverted slightly by the sight of Angelica: small, dark, and frail in her wheelchair. Marcus Cavalli was forgotten completely as the girl's black eyes met her own and glittered with a sudden malevolent intensity.

Chapter Three

"I will not swim, *signorina,* and you cannot persuade me to," Angelica Cavalli avowed, her English stilted and heavily accented. "I do not like to go in the water."

Leigh gazed longingly at the azure waters of the large swimming pool beyond the piazza. With Marcus Cavalli gone for the afternoon, it was the perfect opportunity to shed the stifling brown caftan she wore and go for a refreshing swim. She couldn't do that when he was home, unfortunately, because it was impossible to disguise her shape in the clinging, royal-blue maillot swimsuit she owned. So during each of the three days she had been at Villa Bianca, she had watched enviously from the balcony of her room as Marcus supervised his niece's exercise in the pool. As she had watched she had seen no evidence that Angelica disliked the water. Actually, she had seemed to enjoy herself very much, and with that in mind, Leigh decided to press the issue.

"But I think you do like to swim," she said candidly,

meeting the child's resentful black eyes. "You certainly seem to have a good time when your uncle swims with you."

"But I know that he will not let me drown," Angelica snapped impatiently. "You probably would though."

"Well, I would try very hard not to," Leigh answered with a wry smile, then sighed when she received only a disgusted sneer in return. "Really, you can trust me not to let you drown. I taught swimming classes during my summer holidays from college."

"But that must have been many years ago," Angelica retorted sarcastically, a hint of a malicious smile tugging at the corners of her mouth. "You are so much older now, *signorina.* So I will wait until Marcus can swim with me."

Reluctantly recognizing defeat, Leigh sank back in her chair, searching her brain for something else she and the girl might do together, useless as it probably would be to make any suggestion. Angelica invariably sniffed at her ideas. Leigh was beginning to see that Marcus had been right about his niece—she was a difficult child. Actually, she was nearly impossible, and her personality certainly did not befit her name. She was far from angelic and seemed to find her greatest pleasure in making caustic remarks about anyone who was out of her favor at the moment. Regrettably, Leigh had been out of her favor from the very beginning. Angelica had shown quite blatantly that she resented her new companion and, during the past three days, Leigh had made no progress in dealing with her. Friendly words were as often as not met with stony silence or deliberately insulting remarks. Yet, despite the girl's prickly attitude, Leigh couldn't really dislike her. She was far too pitiful to be disliked. Bitterness and something like defensiveness etched themselves noticeably on the thin dark face, and a very real uncertainty clouded the eyes so similar to her uncle's. It was obvious her unhappiness had to be deep-seated and overwhelming to actually cause hysterical paralysis, and Leigh ached to ease some of her pain. If only she could gain the girl's confidence and her friendship. . . .

"Tell me about your school, Angelica," she said abruptly, unwilling to give up on the child without a fight. "Do you like it or were you glad when it was time for summer vacation?"

"It makes no difference to me whether it is summer or winter," the girl retorted sharply, with an unpleasant little laugh. "Why should it since I was expelled from the convent school in February anyway? Would you like to know why I was expelled, *signorina?* The Mother Superior said my attitude was a bad influence on the other girls and that I would not respond to discipline. Aren't you shocked, *signorina?* Don't you think I am a terrible girl?"

"No, I think you're just like everybody else," Leigh answered matter-of-factly. "All of us have times when we're too upset or too angry to want to obey the rules. We just feel rebellious, but we usually get over that feeling very soon. So I imagine you'll like school again when you go back this autumn."

"I am not ever going back to school again," Angelica announced emphatically, sweeping her hand above her thin lifeless legs. "Why should I? I will never be able to do anything. I am a cripple and someone will always have to look after me."

"You shouldn't think that way," Leigh protested urgently, leaning forward in her chair. "You will walk again someday, I'm sure of it."

"No, I will not! I will not! And don't you tell me that I will!" Angelica cried out suddenly, her face contorted with rage. Her arm shot out and the book she had been holding flew across the piazza, landing on the tile floor with a resounding bang, then sliding over the edge into the bordering carnation bed, crushing several of the soft red blooms. Apparently oblivious to what she had done, she glared at Leigh, her eyes glinting. "You think I could walk now, if I would try, don't you? You are like all the rest! You think I am just pretending that my legs will not move!"

"I don't think you're pretending," Leigh assured her soothingly. "I know your legs really won't move. I only meant that perhaps someday, some doctor will be able to help you to walk again."

"No one can help me. No one will ever be able to help me!" Angelica argued, almost hysterically. "I will never walk again. I am a cripple and someone will always have to take care of me!"

"But even if you never got out of that wheelchair, you would probably be able to take care of yourself," Leigh said gently. "I've known several people who were confined to wheelchairs but they didn't let that stop them from going to school and getting important jobs that they loved. One girl I know works in a hospital lab and she is perfectly capable of taking care of herself. And you could do something important too and, at the same time, look after yourself."

"No, that is a lie! Someone will have to look after me! Someone will!" Angelica cried, nearly in tears. "I will not listen to you, *signorina!*"

As the girl childishly clamped her hands over her ears, Leigh rose swiftly and bent over the wheelchair. With gentle fingers, she pulled Angelica's hands away as she murmured, "I'm sorry I upset you, really I am. Please don't cry. We won't talk about it any more, if you don't want to."

Seemingly infuriated by her own tears, Angelica jerked her hands away to wipe the dampness from her cheeks.

"Go away and leave me alone," she mumbled. "I do not want you here."

Suppressing a sigh, Leigh stepped behind the wheelchair and, after releasing the brake, pushed it down the ramp onto the asphalt walkway that led through the garden.

"We need to be more active," she said, ignoring the child's dismissal. "We spend far too much time on that piazza."

Angelica snorted irritably.

"But I like the piazza, *signorina.*"

"But that doesn't mean we have to put down roots there," Leigh commented casually. "Besides, too much sun isn't good for our skin. We wouldn't want to get wrinkles prematurely, would we?"

"I do not worry about getting wrinkles," the girl answered snidely. "Of course I am not old like you are."

Refusing to be baited, Leigh walked on, pausing occasionally to point out a rose bush, heavy with blossoms or to sniff appreciately the sweet fragrance of the jasmine. Her efforts to draw Angelica into a conversation were futile, however, until they had nearly reached the grape arbor at the bottom of the sloping garden. Then the girl turned in the chair to glare up angrily at her.

"I am tired, *signorina,*" she said crossly. "I want to be taken back to the piazza."

"It's much cooler here in the shade, though, so why don't we stay for a few minutes before starting back," Leigh suggested evenly. "Maybe we can even spot some grapes that are already ripe enough to eat. I've noticed you like them."

The thin hands on the armrests of the chair tightened until the knuckles were white.

"I do not want any grapes now. I want to go back to the piazza," Angelica said stiffly. "I wish you would just leave me alone because I do not need you to stay with me. If I want to be taken somewhere, Marcus can take me."

"Your *Uncle* Marcus is very busy, compiling his next

book. That's why he hired me," Leigh reminded her patiently. "So if you'd just try a little harder to like me, I'm sure we'd both be much happier."

"Take me back to the piazza now, *signorina,*" Angelica commanded haughtily, completely ignoring the friendly overture. "It is too dark here in the shade. I prefer to sit where it is sunny."

Because you know I'm roasting in this ridiculous caftan, Leigh longed to retort, but didn't. Instead, she shrugged nonchalantly and turned the chair back in the direction they had come. Unfortunately, she realized after only a moment that the walkway sloped more steeply that she had imagined. And since the black asphalt was softening in the heat, she was not strong enough to push the chair more than a few yards uphill.

"Well, it looks like I'll have to get Signor Rossetti to help get you to the house," she said, turning back toward the grape arbor. After parking the wheelchair where the walkway levelled off and setting the brake, she smiled down at Angelica. "Just sit right here. I'll be back in a minute."

"I hope so," the girl called out grumpily as she walked away. "I do not like it down here and Marcus will not be pleased that you left me alone."

"It's not the end of the world, so stop trying to make it seem that way," Leigh chided gently though her patience was beginning to wear thin. "I'm sure you'll survive a few minutes alone down here." As a furiously exclaimed string of Italian words followed her up the slope, she smiled ruefully, realizing she was undoubtedly being cursed. It was no wonder to her that Angelica had been expelled from the convent school. Her lack of respect for those in authority would try the patience of even the most saintly of humans.

Hurrying along, Leigh looked around for Signor Rossetti, the housekeeper's gardener husband but, for once, he did not seem to be at his never-ending task of seeking out and destroying weeds. Deciding he must be in the greenhouse, Leigh turned down a path between the rows of crimson oleanders, which led through the small orange grove, but when she peeked into the greenhouse, he wasn't there either.

"Damn, Angelica will be having fits," she muttered, breaking into a run as she crossed the piazza to dash into the salon. Then before her eyes could adjust to the dim indoors, she ran headlong into a solid, unyielding obstacle and nearly lost her balance on collision.

"Where's the fire?" Marcus Cavalli asked, obvious amusement in his voice as his large hands gripped her upper arms to steady her. "Or are you competing in a marathon?"

After fumbling in her pocket for her glasses, Leigh hastily put them on, unaware that mere glass couldn't disguise the soft luminosity in her wide, blue eyes as she gazed up uncertainly at him.

"Oh," she said breathlessly. "I'm sorry. I didn't mean to run you down but—but I guess I just don't see very well without my glasses."

Still holding her arms, Marcus said nothing but as he looked her over from head to toe, his clear, green eyes lingered on the skimpy sandals on her small, slim feet.

Leigh stopped breathing for a moment, wondering what he was thinking. For the past three days she had clumped around in those dreadful black oxfords, but this morning she had refused to wear them and subject her feet to another day of unmitigated torture. She had convinced herself that shoes weren't all that important a detail in her attempt to appear older than she was, but now she wasn't so sure anymore. Why had Marcus seemed so interested in her feet? Afraid to discover why, she quickly diverted his attention.

"I was hurrying to find Signor Rossetti," she explained, her voice embarrassingly shaky. "I've stranded Angelica down at the grape arbor. I—I didn't realize the walk was too steep for me to push her back up. I had to leave her there and I was hoping he would help me get her back up here."

"Rossetti's gone on an errand for me," Marcus told her, removing his hands from her arms at last. "But will I do as a rescuer instead?"

"Of course," she murmured, so disconcerted by the strange way he was smiling at her that she took a jerky step backward and nearly stumbled over a small ivory inlaid table. Her cheeks burned. "Heavens," she said weakly, "I certainly am clumsy today."

"How long have you been in Italy, Miss Sheridan?" he asked, ignoring her embarrassment as he cupped her elbow in his hand to guide her across the piazza and down into the gardens. "All summer?"

"N-Not quite. Only about three weeks actually."

"What made you decide to make it a working holiday, if you don't mind my asking? Surely you didn't get a chance to see all the sights in only two weeks?"

"Well, no, I just—I didn't realize how quickly my money would disappear here," she lied, disgusted with herself for not simply blurting out the truth. Yet, knowing she couldn't risk honesty, she continued, "I'm afraid I just didn't save enough for the trip. But since I didn't want to go back home so soon, I decided to try to find a job here instead. I was really lucky to find a nice, temporary position like this one, though."

"Yes, it had to be temporary, didn't it, so you could get back to the States before school starts in the autumn?" he asked, smiling casually when her eyes darted up to meet his. "Well, I want you to know that I feel Angelica and I are very lucky to have found you too. I think you may be very good for her."

Leigh blushed again, pleased, yet somehow embarrassed by his kind words. "I'm not all that certain I am good for her," she said softly, averting her eyes. "She doesn't like me, you know."

"Give her more time," he counseled. "Angelica is a very confused girl. She finds it hard to trust people until she's had a chance to get to know them."

Not an unwise trait, Leigh thought wryly, almost wishing she had not been so quick to trust Stefano. But then, if she hadn't trusted him, she wouldn't be on the magical isle of Capri at this very moment, walking through a delightful garden with a man as attractive as Marcus Cavalli. So, perhaps something could be said for the mess she had landed herself in. He would never see her as an attractive female, of course, but it was still pleasant to contemplate two months of being in close contact with such an appealing man. It never hurt to dream.

Smiling secretively to herself, she looked up, then suppressed a groan at the look of fury on Angelica's dark face as she watched their approach. Then suddenly, and without warning, sobs were shaking the girl's thin shoulders and Leigh could only stare at her in amazement as Marcus rushed to her side.

"What is it?" he asked urgently, bending down to look into his niece's brown eyes, which were overflowing with tears. "Why are you crying?"

"She left me here all alone and I thought she was never coming back," Angelica sobbed, her voice muffled against her uncle's shirtfront. "She said she would be right back but I've been waiting for nearly an hour."

Leigh's mouth nearly fell open, but as Marcus straightened to stare at her questioningly, she managed to contain her surprise at the lie.

"I haven't been gone more than five minutes, Mr. Cavalli," she assured him softly. "I had only just left her when I found you in the sitting room."

He nodded, seemingly accepting her explaination, but his expression was tender as he turned back to his niece.

"Maybe you just thought Miss Sheridan was gone longer than she actually was," he suggested calmly, releasing the brake of the wheelchair. With astonishing ease, he began pushing the chair up the asphalt walkway, glancing at Leigh as she followed along just behind him. One lean, tanned hand reached out to playfully tousle Angelica's sleek, dark hair. "Don't you think you might have just imagined it was nearly an hour. Time can play tricks on us sometimes."

"No! It was a long time! I didn't imagine it!" the girl argued, craning her neck to glare back at Leigh. Then she broke into a rapid incomprehensible spate of Italian—her accusing tone didn't need translation.

"Speak English, please," Marcus commanded calmly. "Remember, we agreed you needed to practice your English. That's why we were glad we could find you an American companion."

"And you're already speaking it much better," Leigh added, attempting to be supportive. "You were fairly good when I arrived, but now I don't think I notice your accent as much."

Angelica almost snarled back over her shoulder.

"You are a liar, *signorina,*" she said hatefully. "You lie about everything and you are very stupid too."

"That's enough, Angelica," Marcus commanded grimly, stopping the chair halfway up the walk. "You will apologize to Miss Sheridan immediately for your rudeness." And when his niece shook her head belligerently, his jaw tightened. "Apologize at once or you'll be spending the evening alone in your room."

"Oh no, that's all right," Leigh began urgently then halted abruptly as his stern gaze fixed itself on her.

"It is *not* all right, Miss Sheridan."

Leigh wouldn't have argued with him for all the gold in the world, so she merely nodded and looked away.

Unfortunately, Marcus left Angelica and Leigh alone together again after they reached the piazza, and for several minutes the tense silence was broken only by the buzzing of the bees in the flowers and the occasional outburst of song from the birds in the carob trees. Then suddenly, the girl swung her chair around to face Leigh.

"My mother is coming to visit me soon and I do not think she will like finding you here," she announced, thrusting her chin out defiantly. "She is very beautiful, *signorina.* She will make you and your plain hair and your terrible clothes look even more ugly."

At last, Leigh's patience was depleted. Even though Angelica had real emotional problems, that didn't give her the right to take out her misery on other people.

"I've had about enough of you, young lady," she said, her tone calmly authoritative. Sitting up straight in the cushioned patio chair, she wriggled her feet back into her sandals, a no-nonsense gleam in her blue eyes as she held the younger girl's rather startled gaze. "I know you're not a very happy person, but I also know that since I've been here you haven't really tried to be. Well, if you want to waste perfectly nice days, sitting here hating the world and everybody in it—especially me, then I can't stop you. But don't try to drag me down to the miserable depths with you. If you don't like the way I try to deal with you then tell me, but from now on, you will not make any more snide comments about my appearance. In case you didn't know, some people can't help the way they look and it's disgracefully rude of you to take it upon yourself to tell them they are ugly. So you will not tell me that I am again. Is that understood?"

For a moment Angelica could only splutter indignantly, but finally she found her voice. A dark flush rose in her brown cheeks as she clutched the armrests of her chair.

"You would not dare speak to me that way, *signorina,* if Marcus had not defended you a moment ago in the garden. But you are very stupid if you think he will always take your side against me. He loves *me* but you are only a hired servant."

"That may be, but I am still a human being and you'll treat me with respect or I'll have to speak to your uncle about your attitude. And I'm sure he won't tolerate your lack of manners, even though he does love you. And, furthermore, I don't think you should call him Marcus, even when he isn't around to hear you. You should show your respect for him by always calling him *Uncle* Marcus."

"And why should I, *signorina?*" Angelica retorted with a sneer. "Surely you are not so stupid that you have not realized the truth. Marcus is not my uncle. He is my father and I will call him what I please."

"Y-Your father?" Leigh exclaimed chokingly before it dawned on her that the girl could be lying. Then as suspicion mounted, she eyed Angelica warily. "Why would you want me to believe he's your father?" she asked finally. "Do you think I'll let you treat me shabbily if I believe he is?"

"You are so ignorant, *signorina,*" Angelica answered with a disparaging smirk. "You should have guessed I am his daughter before I had to tell you. I look like him, do I not?"

"Well, there's a resemblance, but his brother—"

"His brother married my mother, but Marcus was in love with her too." Angelica sat back in her chair, smiling with smug satisfaction. "They think I do not know the truth but I have heard enough of the servants' gossip to know what really happened. Marcus and Roberto both loved my mother but she chose to marry Roberto. I was born eight months later and Marcus is my father. Why else do you think I would be here, living with him, if I were not? Perhaps I will tell him soon that I know the truth. Then we will not need to go on pretending."

Leigh was speechless. Even as she reminded herself that Angelica had a very vivid imagination, something like an incongruous disillusionment swept over her. What if this story were true? Surely she wouldn't have been immediately and instinctively drawn to a man who could actually deny his own fatherhood. Or could she have been? He was like no man she had ever met before. Perhaps she had been too dazzled by his rugged good looks and obvious intelligence to realize that the real person behind all those attractive traits was not nearly so alluring. She did not like to think she was such a poor judge of character. In fact, she refused to consider that possibility at the moment. Later, when she was over the shock of Angelica's claim, she could sort out her thoughts more calmly.

Jumping up, she hurried over to take the hand grips of Angelica's chair.

"It is getting too warm out here. It's time for your afternoon rest," she said, striving not to show just how ruffled she was. But she was not at all sure how successful she was being when the younger girl tilted back her head and gave her an infuriatingly insolent grin.

As Marcus had threatened, Angelica did indeed spend the evening in her room and since he himself went out for dinner, Leigh was left on her own. After pushing a succulent fillet of sole around and round on her plate for a half-hour or so, she finally gave up on trying to stimulate her appetite. She simply wasn't hungry. So, after apologizing to Signora Rossetti for not doing justice to the meal, she trudged upstairs to her room.

Though it wasn't an unusually warm night, the air seemed oppressive somehow. Feeling as if the walls were closing in, Leigh wandered out onto her balcony, but even out there, she still felt claustrophobic—as if she were confined in a very tiny space. Actually, she was depressed, and she had been depressed since the disturbing little chat with Angelica that afternoon. Thoroughly confused, wondering what she should believe, she had spent the hours before dinner sitting in the chair beside her bed and staring at the fading frescoed panel on the opposite wall. Countless times she had asked herself why she should be so disturbed that Marcus could possibly be Angelica's father, but she hadn't found any answers that she wanted to accept. Finally, she had managed to nearly convince herself that she was disturbed because she didn't like to think he had lied to her.

Yet now, as she stood on the balcony, she was wondering if she had really been honest with herself. Sighing, she gazed at the moonlit garden where shadows of the trees moved stealthily over the ground with each stirring of a gentle breeze. Then, as she watched, someone moved from the darkness into the moonlight that shimmered over the central fountain. It was Marcus—she was certain of it, though he was no more than a broad silhouette in the dim illumination. When her heart inexplicably began to beat in crazy little jerks, she berated herself mentally and turned to go back into her room.

Five minutes later, as she was still wandering about restlessly, trying to decide whether or not it was too early for her bath, Signora Rossetti knocked once on her door then came into the room to tell her the *signor* wished to speak to her in his study.

With extreme reluctance, Leigh went down after checking the tidiness of her confined hair. She hesitated outside his door, smoothing the folds of her dull brown caftan with curiously shaky hands. If only she could appear before him in some decent clothes, she thought wistfully, then as renewed resentment toward Stefano rushed forth, she squared her shoulders and knocked.

When she entered, Marcus was sitting in one of the mammoth, highbacked, leather chairs, but as she walked across the room he got to his feet with lithe, near feline ease, and indicated with a gesture that she should be seated.

Leigh poised herself uneasily on the edge of the sofa, clasping her hands tightly around her knees as she watched him sit down again. The courage she had attained from her re-aroused resentment toward Stefano suddenly deserted her as quickly as it had come, and she could only stare at Marcus and wish it really didn't matter to her what sort of man he might or might not be. Yet, it did matter; she knew it did and admitting that fact to herself made her feel horrendously self-conscious. She felt as if every move she made was being observed and she knew he must be thinking she had to be the world's tackiest frump. He, on the other hand, looked even more unfairly attractive than usual in his dark navy trousers and a light blue cotton polo shirt that stretched taut over the rippling muscles of his shoulders when he moved. Stop thinking of him that way, you imbecile! she told herself hastily, bending her head to avoid meeting his darkly mysterious gaze.

"I wanted to talk to you about Angelica," he began abruptly, his eyes still on her when she looked up again. "I thought I should remind you of what I said about letting her take advantage of you. Judging by what I saw this afternoon, she's becoming very insolent and I don't want her getting the idea she can treat people that way. She may begin to like wielding that sort of power. And if she does, she may never be anxious to let someone help her walk again."

"Can she be helped anyway?" Leigh asked softly. "She's so very bitter."

"I think she wants very much to walk again but she truly believes she can't." Leaning back in his chair, Marcus stretched his long legs out in front of him, stroking his cheek thoughtfully with one finger. "She still thinks she injured her spine during that diving accident that started this entire paralysis business. Not one of the doctors she has seen since then has been able to persuade her that there's absolutely no physical reason why she shouldn't be able to walk; she simply didn't trust them enough to believe they're telling her the truth. But I still think she can be helped eventually, *if* she continues to really want to walk."

"It must be impossible for her to understand how her mind could actually keep her from walking," Leigh said sadly. "After all, she's only a child and she seems to feel all alone."

"Yes, she's lonely; I told you that when you arrived." Leaning forward, Marcus rested his elbows on his knees, allowing his tanned, well-formed hands to relax. "And I was hoping you could ease some of her loneliness, that she would be able to confide in you. If she could only talk to someone. . . ." Pausing, he intently surveyed Leigh's face. "Has she ever shared feelings with you that you think might enable me to help her?"

Leigh gulped, then fought for a deep breath, hoping to slow the wild pounding of her heart. He had just provided her with a perfect opportunity to learn the truth. "Well—uh—she did—" she began haltingly, then knowing what she had to do, she blurted out, "She did tell me that you're really her father, not her uncle."

Marcus' narrowed eyes darkened to a stormy green as he detected the unwittingly accusing note in Leigh's voice. Rising to his feet, he thrust his hands deep into his pockets and came to stand towering over her, his feet planted firmly apart. "And do you believe what she said, Miss Sheridan?" he asked quietly, his gaze roaming slowly over her. "Do you think I am her father?"

Uncertain of what she believed, she looked up into

his dark lean face with wide bewildered eyes. "I-I really don't know what to think now," she confessed squeakily, wishing he wasn't so damned big or so overwhelmingly close. "Are—Are you her father?"

"No," he answered emphatically and without hesitation. "I am not Angelica's father. But I can understand why she's obviously decided to pretend I am. I'm sorry to say my brother, Roberto, isn't exactly a model parent and, worse yet, Angelica's mother, Sophia, doesn't seem all that interested in her either." He grimaced, raking his fingers through the dark thickness of his hair. "To be honest, Miss Sheridan, both of Angelica's parents are rather immature. You see, their marriage was a necessity after a brief summer romance. He was nineteen; she was seventeen—both far too young to work diligently at making their marriage work. Right after Angelica was born, they separated. Roberto decided to be an international playboy, who impresses his women by risking his life in race cars in the summer, and on the ski slopes in the winter. Sophia, despite her strict upbringing, is now a sophisticated, pleasure seeking jet-setter. So you may understand now why their daughter wants to say I'm her father. At least, at the moment, I'm living in the same house with her."

Though Leigh had not been aware she was holding her breath as he spoke, it now released in a sigh as relief washed over her. She smiled up at him rather shyly, unaware of how young and vulnerable she looked at that moment. "You really told me the truth then," she murmured unnecessarily. "I'm glad."

He reached down to take her hands and pull her up to stand before him, so close that their bodies were almost touching. And at her soft intake of breath, he gripped her upper arms lightly, his thumbs moving in small disturbing circles against the linen fabric of her sleeves.

"Did you really think I might have lied to you?" he asked softly, an odd, appealing huskiness in his deep voice. "Surely you knew I would have told you if Angelica were really my daughter? Didn't you?"

"Yes. No. I mean, I don't know," she answered breathlessly. "I—I don't really know you."

"Maybe we can remedy that in the next few weeks," he murmured, cupping her face in large yet infinitely gentle hands. His darkening eyes moved slowly over her delicate features before his fingers began their own slow exploration and when she trembled as one appealingly rough fingertip brushed across her lips, causing them to part with a soft little gasp, he lowered his head. His warm breath mingled with hers as he whispered, "You're a very intriguing woman, Leigh. I suspect there's much more to you than meets the eye."

"Oh no—no, there isn't. Really," she protested hastily, fearing he was beginning to see through her disguise. "I—I'm really exactly what I seem to be."

"No, I don't think that's true," he disagreed with a disconcerting smile, reaching up without warning to remove her large-framed glasses, then dropping them behind her onto the soft sofa cushion. "Why do you wear those? What are you trying to hide?"

"N—Nothing, nothing at all, really." Shivering violently as his thumbs stroked the soft brown arches of her brows, she closed her eyes, hoping to negate the sudden longing she felt to be kissed. But the longing only intensified.

"Look at me, Leigh," he commanded softly. "You can't hide by closing your eyes. I still know what a beautiful blue they are."

Obeying reluctantly, she gazed up at him, thoroughly bewildered and more than a little afraid. He was dangerous enough normally, but with him in this coaxingly provocative mood, she knew she could be playing with fire. Without much success, she tried to smile nonchalantly and pulled his hands away from her face. But he caught her small fingers in his, lifting them for a devastating instant to touch against his lips before he released them.

"I'd like to photograph you sometime," he said, his dark gaze holding hers. "Would you be willing?"

At the moment, she feared she would be willing to accept any proposition he made and the thought was so disturbing that she forgot to answer his question.

"Well, would you?" he persisted. "Or are you camera shy?"

"Oh, you know you don't want to photograph me," she protested weakly, grimacing as she tugged at the brown caftan. "I—I'm so plain."

"I have a feeling that just the wrapper is plain," he responded with a wry smile. "Am I right?"

Shaking her head rather too emphatically, she moved away from the enticing warmth emanating from his body.

"I—I'm tired," she lied dismally, edging toward the door. "I—I think I'd better go to my room. Goodnight, Mr. Cavalli."

Before he had a chance to react, she made her escape, nearly stumbling several times as she ran up the stairs. And it wasn't until she was safely in her own room, when she caught sight of her reflection in the mirror, that she began to suspect she had just allowed herself to be conned. Drab as she looked, she couldn't imagine how Marcus Cavalli could be attracted to her at all, even slightly. And maybe he wasn't. Maybe he had simply been trying to charm her into believing that he wasn't Angelica's father. He had told her he wasn't, *then* had immediately taken her mind off his niece by that near seduction scene. Had he staged it for that very reason?

Leigh didn't know. As she sat down on the edge of the bed and wrapped her arms tightly around her waist, she only knew that Marcus Cavalli could prove to be a very dangerous man. If that had been a deliberate display of his charm that she had experienced downstairs, she could be in very deep trouble. Unlike Stefano, Marcus had shown a subtle and an infinitely more potent expertise in the art of seduction.

Chapter Four

Early Sunday afternoon, Leigh sat on a bench on the quay at Marina Grande, staring at her feet sliding in and out of her backless leather sandals. It had been a long, hot, tiring week and it was a relief to leave the Villa Bianca for a few hours and be her real self again. At least, she would be able to become her real self when Stefano arrived on the launch from Naples and they went on to the beach at Marina Piccola where she could finally change from the garbardine tent she was wearing to her mailiot swimsuit. She could hardly wait. Since her disturbing scene with Marcus Tuesday night, the dresses she was forced to wear had become even more obnoxious to her. She had decided that he had simply been playing with her, perhaps hoping to charm her by adding a little spice to the drab, unexciting life he undoubtedly believed she led. Humiliated by his patronizing actions, she now longed to appear before him, just once, dressed in decent clothes and looking her very best. It was tantalizing to imagine what his reaction might be if he saw her in a dress that accentuated her shape instead of concealing it. With her hair loose around her shoulders, she would look so much better that he would stare at her in open-mouth disbelief. If only she could shock him with such a transformation perhaps her ego would begin to recover from the bruising it had taken Tuesday night. Yet, she knew very well she was merely daydreaming. She knew she did not dare discard her disguise. It was almost a cinch Marcus would fire her if he learned exactly how young she was. Job security had to take precedence over the soothing of a bruised ego.

Pushing her huge glasses back up on the bridge of her nose, Leigh gazed with a pensive smile at the violent red bougainvillaea that clung to a trellis by a small whitewashed house up the hillside from the harbor. Everything here on Capri seemed much more vivid than in other places. Colors were brighter and the fragrance of the abundant flowers was sweeter, even emotions seemed far more intense. At least that was a good rationalization for her reaction to Marcus Cavalli. She was simply too caught up in the magical atmosphere.

Lost in thought for a moment, Leigh barely noticed the throbbing roar of an engine; then the irritating noise penetrated her consciousness and she looked up to find Stefano easing his red Ferrari off the narrow road that led from the ferry slip past the quay. After cutting the engine, he swung himself over the closed door on the driver's side and bounded up the wooden steps of the pier.

"Come along, Leigh. Let's get you to the beach and out of that horrible dress," he said without a trace of shame as he reached her side. And as he escorted her to his car, he chattered on, "How was your week? Did you miss me as much as I missed you? Tell me about the people you are working for."

Without bothering to respond to the rapid-fire

inquisition, Leigh gave Stefano several thoroughly disgusted glances as they drove away from the quay. If she had any pride at all she would refuse to go to the beach with him, but at the moment, protesting his cavalier attitude seemed far less important than shedding the hot gabardine caftan for the next few hours. Actually, that was the only reason she had called Stefano and asked him to meet her here today. She hadn't wished to risk attracting the unwanted attention of some of the more brazen young men who would assume a girl alone on a beach was fair game. So Stefano had his uses after all, which was only fair, considering all the times he had tried to use her.

On the other side of the island, Marina Piccola was a steep pebbly beach dotted with small boats, and decorated occasionally with vibrant purple or scarlet bougainvillaea vines. The beach was crowded with sun-worshipers while the rock-scattered blue waters drew the more energetic visitors into the creaming surf. Leigh was rather relieved there were plenty of people about. Considering Stefano's wandering hands, she certainly wouldn't have wanted to spend the afternoon with him on a lonely, secluded stretch of sand.

As she wriggled into her swimsuit in one of the striped tents the bathing establishment provided for that purpose, Leigh felt a delicious sense of freedom. Except at night, alone in her room, she had endured the hot confining folds of the caftans for over a week now. It was wonderful to step out into the sunshine and feel a gentle breeze against her bare arms and legs. As she stepped gingerly down the sloping stony beach to where Stefano stood waiting, she made a half-serious resolution to never wear long sleeves again in her life—after she left Villa Bianca.

As Leigh approached, Stefano pursed his lips in a small *moue* of disappointment. "Do you realize I have never seen you in a bikini?" he said immediately, gesturing vaguely toward the sunbathers on the beach.

"Surely you would not have felt self-conscious wearing one here—all the other girls are."

"I'm sorry you don't like the way I look," she responded without much genuine concern. "But I happen to prefer this suit to a bikini."

Stefano grinned cheekily. "I did not say I disliked the way you looked. I only meant I wish I could see more of you."

"This is all of me I care to show, thank you," she retorted, grinning back. "Now, let's find a spot to put down our towels. I can't wait a moment longer to get in that water."

For the most part, Leigh did the swimming while Stefano sat sunning himself on a partially submerged rock, watching her. And though he seemed to be getting a little impatient for her to come out of the water and talk to him, she simply couldn't force herself to leave the delicious coolness of the gentle waves. Several times she swam out with long, easy strokes, then allowed the sea to sweep her back toward shore. Then she would tread shallower water for a while, or float on her back, or dive occasionally to the sandy bottom in water so clear she could see every pebble and shell. After nearly an hour, however, her limbs began to ache and she swam to the rock where Stefano sat waiting, and climbed up to join him reluctantly.

As she squeezed the excess water from her thick braid of hair, she smiled slightly, gazing out at the distant Faraglioni, those familiar, tall, rock-pinnacles that jutted out of the sea just off shore. "It's nice here," she commented softly. "The water really feels great."

"The beach is too crowded," Stefano complained, his tone slightly sullen, as his eyes swept over the entire length of her body. "I think we should go for a drive somewhere and be alone. We have not seen each other for over a week."

Leigh tried to soften her refusal with a genuine smile. "Let's just stay here, please. I don't think I can tear myself away from this water until I've had another chance to go in. Do you know this is the first time I've felt really cool since I arrived on Capri? Those caftans are the hottest things I've ever worn."

With a stiff, begrudging nod, Stefano gave in, but after helping her down off the rock, he caught her hand as they waded back onto the beach, releasing it reluctantly when she sank down onto her knees on their thick beach towel. Then, after putting on sunglasses, he stretched out beside her as she smoothed tanning lotion over her arms. Propping himself up on his elbows, he watched her for a long moment, then reached out to brush his fingers over her creamy smooth thigh with a suggestive smile. "Shall I put some of that lotion on your legs for you?"

"No, thank you," she murmured, moving out of reach of his exploring hand. "I can manage the legs fine but I might need you to help me with my back."

"Amare mia," he was whispering a moment later, easing the straps of her swimsuit off her shoulders. As he began to rub the tanning lotion over her back, his hands almost immediately started to roam a bit too familiarly and when his fingertips moved to where they could brush the curve of her breast, she stiffened.

"Stefano, don't. You know I don't like you to do that," she said as nicely as she could—considering the fact that she had always hated being manhandled. Removing his hand, she shook her head chidingly at him. "Let's just make this a nice relaxing afternoon, all right? No romantic ideas. Only conversation."

With an impatient groan, he fell back down onto the towel, flinging his arm up to cover his eyes in a tragic pose; when she paid no attention to his theatrics for a minute or so, he propped himself up again. "All right, if you want to talk to much, tell me about this girl you're taking care of. Is she a nice child?"

"She has problems, as you well know, Stefano," Leigh answered reprovingly. "You shouldn't have conveniently forgotten to tell me she was confined to a wheelchair."

"But I thought I did tell you that!" he exclaimed innocently, his expression growing sulky, as if she had wounded his feelings terribly by suggesting he had not told her the entire truth. "If I did not mention it, I assure you, it was an oversight. Why should I deliberately keep such information from you?"

"Because you knew I might not take the job if I realized I would be dealing with a child suffering with hysterical paralysis. I would have been afraid I wasn't competent enough to deal with her problem. *And* you knew Marc—Mr. Cavalli—that's Angelica's uncle—wanted to hire someone who had experience with disturbed children."

"Wait, *cara!*" Stefano exclaimed, grasping her arm roughly. "Did you start to say Marcus? Marcus Cavalli? Do you mean to tell me you're working for *the* Marcus Cavalli, the photographer?"

"Well, yes," Leigh said, wrinkling her brow confusedly. "But why should that surprise you so much?"

Staring at her in disbelief, Stefano began to wave his arms about excitedly as he explained, "Don't you know what is going on in the world, *cara?* What kind of reporter are you? You should know that Cavalli's whereabouts have been unknown for the past three months! *Dio mio!* You have been sitting on top of a story some reporters would kill for, and you did not even know it!"

"But what story? Why is everybody so interested in Marcus Cavalli's whereabouts? What's made him such a hot news item?"

"Dio, you really do not know what is going on in the world, do you?" Stefano exclaimed rather insultingly. *"Cara,* Cavalli was involved for several weeks with Brandi Wilkins. Surely even you know who she is—Hollywood's brightest new starlet?"

"Well, of course I know who she is," Leigh answered impatiently. "But how could he have been involved with her? I thought she was married."

Stefano lifted his eyes heavenward. "You innocent! She *is* married! That was the problem. She and Cavalli were seeing a great deal of each other, but they say her husband was not simply ignoring their relationship as most men do. Instead, they say he was considering suing for divorce, citing Cavalli as corespondent. That's done so seldom these days that it stirred up quite a scandal when the rumor got out. Then Brandi went into seclusion in a hotel suite in Paris and Cavalli simply disappeared. But you have found him, *amare mia!* And you now have the chance to write the story of your career!"

"What?" she exclaimed incredulously. "Are you out of your mind? I'm not at Villa Bianca to write a story. I was hired as a companion and I can't divulge information about the family's personal affairs. There's no way I would write a story about Marcus. If he wanted his whereabouts known, he would get in touch with someone in the press."

"Marcus, is it? And how did he get to be Marcus to you?" Stefano asked, jealousy flashing in his eyes as a flush crept into his cheeks beneath his tan. "Hmm, *cara mia?* Tell me how you and Marcus Cavalli got acquainted on a first-name basis?"

His insinuating tone infuriated Leigh and, as she glared at him disgustedly, the color rose in her cheeks also. "If you're implying I'm involved in some sort of romance with Marcus Cavalli, then you're crazy as a loon! Wearing those horrendous clothes you bought me, how could I possibly attract the attention of any man?"

Without answering that question, Stefano veered off in another direction. "But that does not mean you are not attracted to him, does it?" he countered crossly.

"Are you, Leigh? Most other women find him nearly irresistible. So why should I believe you are any different from others of your gender?"

"I refuse to discuss this ridiculous topic a minute longer," she declared stiffly, turning away from him with a toss of her head. Yet, something akin to shame was writhing inside her. She had always been willing to admit it when she had made a mistake and it was totally out of character for her to deny that she had been foolishly attracted to Marcus. Yet, she simply couldn't admit her gullibility. It was beyond her capabilities to confess she had been taken in by the worst kind of playboy, the kind who chased after other men's wives and then ran away and hid at the first bit of trouble.

Since Marcus was obviously so untrustworthy, it was only logical for Leigh to assume he had also lied about not being Angelica's father. Yet, that idea was so depressing that it didn't bear thinking about at the moment. Trying to push it far back in her mind, she lay back on the towel and closed her eyes against the glaring sun, nearly forgetting Stefano was sitting there beside her.

He, however, never allowed himself to be forgotten for long. Turning onto his side, he whispered into her ear: "I am sorry, *amare mia*. I should not have spoken to you that way. But I am just very jealous."

As his lips touched Leigh's shoulder and his hand spread possessively across her abdomen, her eyes flew open. "Didn't I just tell you not to touch me that way?" she whispered irritably. "Now stop it, Stefano, or I'm going back to the villa."

As she brushed his hand away, he got up quickly, glowering down at her. "I will go buy drinks," he muttered, then walked away.

Stefano's news had been so disconcerting that Leigh was too preoccupied to pay him much attention when he returned with two iced drinks. After a few sips of the fruity concoction, she excused herself abstractedly and went for another long swim in the sea. Her deflection only served to make him all the more sullen and the remainder of the afternoon passed in a tense, uncomfortable silence that was broken only occasionally by a stiff comment by one or the other of them. In the end, it proved to be a day off that was not worth the paper it would take to write home about.

On Monday evening, after a long refreshing bath, Leigh donned her briefest, sheerest cotton gown and sat down at the vanity to take down her hair, but before she could remove the first pin from the tight chignon, there was a soft knock on her door.

"One moment, Signora Rossetti," she called out, jumping up to grab her white eyelet robe from the end of the bed. Thrusting her arms into the short sleeves she began frantically to do the buttons, but as she was fumbling with the third one, the door opened and, incredibly, Marcus stepped into the room. Leigh's fingers froze as she gasped, "Mr. Cavalli! What—"

"I want to talk to you," he said, his expression unreadable as his gaze flicked over her. "This can't wait."

"Is—is something wrong?" she asked, willing herself to finish buttoning the robe, which was voluminous enough to make her appear shapeless. "Is it Angelica?"

"This has nothing to do with my niece." After closing the door firmly behind him, he walked slowly toward Leigh, his dark enigmatic gaze holding hers as he stopped so close in front of her that she had to tilt her head back to look up at him. He smiled suddenly but it was an oddly taunting smile. "I thought you might be interested in knowing I went out shooting yesterday. Shooting photographs, I mean—at Marina Piccola."

Leigh's eyes widened behind her sham glasses then quickly darted away to stare blindly beyond his broad shoulders. "Marina Piccola?" she repeated squeakily, alternate waves of burning heat and icy cold sweeping over her entire body. "I—I'm afraid I don't understand what that's suppose to mean to—to me."

"I think you understand perfectly but if you need reminding, take a look at this," he commanded, his voice deceptively soft, as he held out a large manila envelope. "Take it."

"But—"

"Take it and open it."

Too frightened by now to dare disobey, Leigh reached out for the envelope and her trembling fingers felt curiously numb as they closed on the smooth brown paper. As she fumbled with the tucked-in flap, her eyes sought his involuntarily, but the words she might have spoken halted in her throat at the relentless intensity of his gaze. Swallowing convulsively, she slipped her fingers inside the envelope and slowly removed a brilliant color photograph, barely able to suppress the groan that rose in her throat when she recognized herself. The camera had caught her at the worst possible moment, as she was lying on the towel on the beach, every shapely contour of her body accentuated by the clinging swimsuit. Her eyes were closed, and Marcus had snapped the picture just as Stefano had brushed his lips against her shoulder and spread his hand across her abdomen—only a fraction of a second before she had glared up at him and pushed away his hand. She actually looked as if she welcomed Stefano's caresses! There was something sensuous about the expression on her face, and she now wondered, bleakly, what she had been thinking about at that moment to make her look that way. Yet, the girl in the photo bore such a little resemblance to the reflection she had been seeing in the mirror for the past ten days that she couldn't understand how Marcus had made the connection. Or maybe he hadn't really. Maybe he had simply seen a slight resemblance, which had aroused his suspicion and he had come here tonight, hoping he would learn the truth. Maybe he really didn't *know* it was her. So maybe if she bluffed. . . . She forced herself to look at him.

"I—I'm afraid I still don't understand," she managed to say with admirable calm. "Is—Is this picture supposed to mean something to me?"

"Oddly enough, taking that photo was really a spur of the moment decision," he said softly, as if he hadn't even heard her attempted bluff. "I was some distance away when the contrasting skin tones caught my attention—the man so dark and the girl with only a hint of a light tan. I zoomed in with the lens, but even then, I was more interested in capturing the nearly pearl-like shimmer of light on the girl's skin than I was in her face. It was only tonight when I was making the prints that I realized I had photographed you."

"But that isn't me! Oh, how ridiculous! I don't even look . . ."

"Then I assume you have a twin sister living on Capri?"

"Of course not! I don't have a sister anywhere! And I can't imagine why you think the girl in this picture is me or a twin! I don't look like that picture at all. That girl is—and—I'm so—so, well, you know, so much plainer."

Shaking his head, Marcus slipped the photograph from her fingers and dropped it carelessly onto the vanity before gripping her shoulders to draw her closer.

"Oh, it's you all right, Leigh," he whispered mockingly as he unfastened the first button of her robe, then the second. "You see, I've known all along that you weren't the shapeless young woman you seem to be at first glance. I have a photographer's eye, remember? I see little details like slim ankles, delicate wrists and cheeks with appealing little hollows."

Nearly hypnotized by the sound of his voice and the dark, mysterious look in his eyes, Leigh was unaware that he had completely unbuttoned her robe until his hard hands spanned her waist, warming her sensitive skin through the thin fabric of her gown. Her breath caught in her throat and she tried to pull away, but it was useless.

"I knew you were hiding something underneath those shrouds you've been wearing," he continued, ignoring her attempted escape. "But do you know what I imagined you wanted to conceal? It's amusing, actually. I thought you might be three or four months pregnant and in such a need of money that you were hiding your pregnancy so you could keep this job. But you're not pregnant, are you, Leigh?" he whispered close to her ear. His right hand slid slowly across her flat abdomen, pressing down lightly, intimately. "No, you couldn't be. You weren't hiding a pregnancy. You were hiding this exquisite body, and that could be considered a sin. You shouldn't hide something so lovely."

"Don't," she whispered back, appalled by the feelings his hands on her were arousing. "Please don't."

His lips brushed teasingly against her neck as he muttered, "Don't what?"

"Don't—don't *touch* me!"

"Ah, but I have to. I want to know exactly what you're like." Drawing away slightly, he reached up to remove the glasses she wore. "I was fairly sure these weren't to correct a vision problem. You seemed to see very well without them." After laying them on the vanity, he smiled down lazily at her and his hands moved around to pull the pins from the chignon knotted on the nape of her slender neck. As her hair tumbled down in golden disarray, his fingers tangled in the silky softness, and he brought a few strands forward on each side to lay over her shoulders. Gentle fingertips explored the delicate hollow at the base of her throat as his darkening eyes narrowed. "So this is the real Leigh. Lovely—much too lovely to resist."

"No!" she gasped, as his hands sought her breasts.

With a soft, fearful cry, she stepped back jerkily, her legs weak and trembling as she looked up at him with wide, reproachful eyes.

"All right, now that I have your undivided attention, suppose you tell me why you were so anxious to come to work here," he asked abruptly, a threatening note in his voice. "Or is the answer to that obvious? Are you here to spy on me? How the hell did you know where I was in the first place?"

"But I didn't know!" Leigh's cheeks paled as she suddenly understood what he meant. He was in hiding, and now he was assuming she was one of those celebrity-chasers who never gave anybody even a little famous a chance to have a moment's privacy. And if he learned she had worked for a newspaper, he would be certain that was what she was. Somehow she had to make him believe that she hadn't come here to pry into his personal life. Searching his face for some sign that he would be willing to listen, she felt a mounting dread when she only encountered an icy stare, and when his jaw tightened, she gestured helplessly. "Please believe me, I didn't even know your name when I accepted this job, so I couldn't have come here to spy on you."

"But you must have had some reason for this little masquerade," he countered harshly. With one long stride, he was close to her, gripping her shoulders with rough impatience. "If you didn't come here to spy, why was this job so important to you?"

"I—I either had to go to work or leave Italy and I—"

"And you couldn't bear the thought of leaving your young lover behind, is that it?"

"No, that's not it at all!" she protested vehemently, her cheeks flooding with crimson color. "I—I don't even have a lover."

"And what do you call that young man in the photograph?" Marcus retorted cuttingly, glancing with distaste at the picture laying on the vanity. "Surely you're not going to try to make me believe he's just a friend of yours? The way he has his hands all over you suggests something far different from a merely friendly relationship. Besides, I remember the little scene in front of the camera shop in Rome. You thought I would forget that, didn't you? He had his hands all over you then too."

"Oh, Stefano's always pawing me and I'm forever asking him to stop it."

A mocking light illuminated Marcus' green eyes. "That's not exactly the way your young man tells it."

Leigh's eyes widened in surprised confusion. "What do you mean that isn't the way he tells it? I don't understand what you're saying."

"I'm saying, my dear Miss Sheridan, that you've gotten yourself involved with one of those immature young men, who brags about his conquests," Marcus answered sarcastically. "I happened to be buying a drink Sunday when your Stefano sauntered in off the beach and began to regale a friend of his with the story of his torrid romance with an uninhibited American girl, namely, you."

"He didn't?" she gasped, her cheeks paling again. Without thinking, she clutched Marcus' arm imploringly, then dropped her hand hastily when she felt the taut muscles beneath her fingers. She shook her head disbelievingly. "How could he do that? How could he go around telling such—"

"Such intimate secrets? Very indiscreet of him, isn't it? But he is just a boy," Marcus said softly, lowering his head to brush firm lips across her cheeks toward her mouth. And when she struggled instinctively, he hauled her into his arms, holding her fast against him with very little effort. He smiled down at her suggestively. "You deserve better than a little boasting boy like him, my lovely Leigh. You deserve a man who doesn't broadcast his affairs far and wide. And I can assure you I can be the very soul of discretion."

Leigh's heart seemed to leap up into her throat as he

tilted her chin up and his mouth hovered just above her own. The supplication in her wide eyes did nothing to alter the relentless glimmer in his. When he bent his head lower and his warm breath caressed her lips, she panicked and tried to wrench free. But his arms tightened like bands around her, preventing escape.

"Please. Mr. Cavalli, I—"

"Marc," he whispered. "Since our relationship is about to change, I think you can call me Marc."

What did he mean? Leigh's heart seemed to stop then began to thud wildly. "Mr. Cavalli, I—"

"Marc, Leigh," he coaxed. "Say it. Say my name."

"I can't," she insisted, pressing her hands against his firm chest, curling her fingers into the soft thin fabric of his shirt. "L-Let me go, please."

"But I don't want to let you go," he muttered, sliding his fingers into her tousled hair as his thumb brushed slowly back and forth across her tightly closed mouth. Whispering her name softly, he pressed the thumb into her chin just beneath the full curve of her lower lip and tugged her mouth open slightly, probing her inner lip's tender, veined flesh until she trembled violently. Then his mouth took possession of hers.

Leigh moaned softly as a flicker of sensual delight ignited every nerve in her body, until every inch of her was aching to be touched. No one had ever made her feel the way Marc was making her feel, and her arms slid up to encircle the strong tanned column of his neck. Her breasts yielded to the muscular line of his chest, heightening the delight, and she twined her fingers in the thick springy hair on his nape. As his tongue explored the sweet softness of her lips, then slipped inside the opening flower of her mouth, his invasion aroused desires in her she had never before experienced.

With innocent, reckless fervor, she pressed herself closer, finding her satisfaction in his hard marauding kisses and in the powerful arms wrapped tightly round her waist; she was not yet aware that what they were now sharing was not nearly enough to satisfy him.

That devastating realization, however, came almost immediately. His seeking fingers probed her spine down to the tantalizing arch between slim waist and the gentle, outward curve of her hips. His hands tenderly closed on her firm flesh, pressing her against him.

Leigh's legs nearly collapsed beneath her, and her breath was expelled in a soft, frightened gasp as he forced her awareness of his stirring masculine desire that surged hard and strong against her abdomen. She had never before allowed any man to hold her as Marc was, and with a sudden realization that she must resist, she began to squirm frantically in his arms. But her struggling, rather than deterring him, only seemed to arouse him more.

"No! Oh, Marc, please," she begged, terrified of the overwhelming weakness that sapped her legs of all strength. "I can't—I don't—"

"Hush, hush," he whispered coaxingly, nibbling her lips then covering them roughly with his as he slipped her robe from her shoulders, down her slender arms. As the cotton eyelet fell to the floor at their feet, he swept her up in his arms and carried her to her bed to put her down gently. Emerald green eyes held hers as he quickly shed his shirt. Then he was on the bed with her, bearing her slight body down into the softness of the mattress with the evocative weight of his body.

As firm, seeking lips claimed hers again, her hands involuntarily brushed the fine dark hair on his chest, and her fingers traced the outline of his shoulders' corded muscles. She was lost once more, swept away by passions she had never really believed existed. All she wanted was to be touched by him forever, and she trembled with delight as his hands slipped under her gown, over her hips, lingering for a moment on the sensitized skin of her waist, then moving up to cover her breasts.

"God, your skin's like satin," he muttered huskily, tracing light fingertips around the aroused, swollen peaks. His lips trailed a blazing path along her neck, over her shoulders, down toward her straining breasts.

As she realized what he was about to do, she also realized with quickening panic that he was not Stefano, who could be deterred with a curt word and a rap on the hand. And she knew if she didn't resist Marc now, he might not allow her to resist him later. She pushed at his chest.

"No. No, please stop. I—I can't let you," she cried softly. "Marc, please. I'm sorry."

"Don't stop me, Leigh," he whispered hoarsely, squeezing her breasts with strong compelling hands. "You want me as much as I want you."

"But—But I can't!"

Perhaps it was her voice breaking that persuaded him. Lifting his head, he gazed down at her small face, his eyes glimmering with passion. Then suddenly, with a muffled exclamation, he sat up on the edge of the bed, his back to her, as he raked his fingers through his dark hair.

"How old are you really?" he muttered. "Seventeen, eighteen, what? It's fairly obvious you're nowhere near as old as I was told you were."

"I—I—you—"

"How old, Leigh?"

"Twenty-five," she lied impetuously. "I'm twenty-five."

He glanced back at her, his expression unreadable.

"Twenty-five," he repeated flatly. "A very young twenty-five then. Or are you one of those old-fashioned girls who only has one lover in her life at a time? That's a quality I might find admirable under different circumstances. As it is though—"

"But that isn't it! Stefano's not—"

"Never mind," Marc said curtly, rising to his feet. "You have every right to remain faithful to your *boy*friend, if that's what you want. But just don't expect to play this little game with me again—because the next time we progress this far, you'll get more than you bargained for, I promise you."

He snatched up his shirt and slipped it on as he strode to the door. Leigh sat up, clutching her pillow before her like a shield.

"I-I'll leave tomorrow," she said weakly. "As early as I can."

Turning back, Marc stared at her mockingly, shaking his head.

"You're staying, Leigh," he announced harshly. "Too many people have already run out on Angelica. But *you* won't. Is that understood?"

Biting her lips, she nodded unhappily, and when he went out and closed the door firmly behind him, she flung herself down on the bed, hiding her burning face in her pillow. Suddenly, she was very scared. Marc had aroused in her a passionate side of her nature that she had never dreamed existed. And, once aroused, it might never be easily suppressed, especially if he ever chose to touch her again.

Chapter Five

Early the next afternoon, Leigh stood at a small table on the piazza, trying, without much success, to interest Angelica in arranging a large bouquet of blue Canterbury bells in a vase.

"Where did you get that dress, *signorina?*" the younger girl asked abruptly, far less interested in arranging flowers than in Leigh's overnight metamorphosis. She frowned perplexedly, her black eyes conveying a hint of envy as they closely examined the sleeveless green cotton jersey Leigh wore. "And why have you taken down your hair? Where are your eyeglasses?"

Stepping back to survey the vaseful of flowers, Leigh smiled. She had been wondering when Angelica would start asking questions. Since breakfast, when she had gasped aloud at her first sight of Leigh, she had stubbornly managed to contain her curiosity. But now, at last, after a valiant effort, she was succumbing.

"The way I looked before was sort of a disguise," Leigh explained vaguely, lifting up one delicately blossomed stem in her arrangement to perfect its symmetry. Then, turning, she smiled rather sheepishly at the girl in the wheelchair. "You see, your uncle wanted an older companion for you, but a friend of mine managed to get me the job through an acquaintance of his at the employment agency. They never saw me and I didn't know someone older was expected until about two hours before I was to arrive here. So the only thing I could do was to try to look older."

Angelica's black eyes widened. "But were you not afraid to play such a trick, *signorina?*" she asked, a certain amount of awed respect in her voice. "What if your disguise had not fooled us? Oh, I would never be courageous enough to try what you did."

"Well, I have to admit I was very nervous, especially at first," Leigh said, settling herself on the lounger beside Angelica's chair. "But I needed this job, so I decided to take the chance."

Angelica leaned forward to whisper conspiratorially. "But why are you not disguised again today? I think perhaps you should go change back to your old clothes before my—my Papa sees you this way. He may be very angry at you for deceiving him."

"And I think you should call Mr. Cavalli Uncle Marcus, instead of Papa," Leigh said gently. "Unless you want to start calling him Papa to his face. That would be more respectful."

Angelica's olive complexion paled several shades as she shook her head. "Oh, but I could not call him Papa, n-not yet," she stammered. "Remember, he does not think I know he is my father." The uncertain look in her eyes intensified for a brief instant, then slowly faded as curiosity reasserted itself. "But you did not answer my question: Why are you not disguised today? Are you not afraid of what Marcus will do to you when he learns how you have tricked him?"

"Your uncle already knows I'm not as old as I pretended to be."

"He knows?" Angelica exclaimed softly. "And you are still here, *signorina?* Marcus can get very angry sometimes. I am very surprised he did not get angry enough with you to send you away."

"Oh, he got angry enough, believe me," Leigh said with a rueful little smile. "But he decided to let me stay here with you anyway."

"But I still do not understand how he knew you were deceiving him," the younger girl mused. "I did not ever imagine you were really so pretty and so slim. Those ugly clothes that you wore made you look so—so—what is the word—so—"

"Dumpy?"

"Si, *signorina,* that is it. You looked very dumpy. So how did Marcus know that you are not that way at all?"

Leigh shifted uncomfortably on the lounger, wondering how she could change the subject without doing it too obviously. All morning she had been trying to forget the events of last night, so she wasn't especially eager to explain how Marcus had guessed her secret. And she was even less eager to be reminded of the consequences she had suffered because he had. Luckily, at the moment, a flurry of activity from inside the sitting room claimed Angelica's attention, and with the sudden, rapid tapping of heels on the tiled piazza floor, and curious both she and Leigh turned around.

"*Mama!* You have come to see me!" Angelica cried joyously at the sight of the elegant young woman who approached. Wheeling her chair around, she started for her mother. "Oh, I am so glad you are here! I have been wanting you to come."

"*Bambina mia,*" Sophia Cavalli cooed, taking her daughter's thin shoulders and leaning down to brush a kiss across her cheek. But when Angelica impulsively wrapped her arms around her neck and held her fast, a flicker of impatience briefly tightened her jaw. "Take care, *bambina,"* she chided, with a fake little laugh. "If you do not break my neck, you will most certainly muss my hair."

"Oh, *scusa,* Mama, I am so sorry," Angelica cried, hastily disentangling her arms to sit back in her chair, a smile of pure ecstasy lighting her face.

Her mother smiled back at her, rather uneasily. Then at last she noticed Leigh, and a small frown creased her brow, marring an otherwise flawless dark complexion. She inclined her head in a stiff nod.

Immediately, Leigh rose to her feet and extended her hand. "I am Angelica's companion, Signora Cavalli," she introduced herself. "Leigh Sheridan."

After responding with a rather weak handshake, the older woman allowed her curious gaze to sweep slowly over Leigh. "When I talked with Marc two days ago, he told me he had engaged a companion for my daughter, but somehow I received the impression that you were older."

Leigh blushed as Angelica giggled merrily.

"The *signorina* was older two days ago, Mama. But she was wearing—"

"How have you been feeling, *bambina?"* Sophie Cavalli interrupted as if she did not hear. Patting her perfectly coiffed short black hair with the crimson-tipped fingers of one hand, she sat down and, after crossing her trim ankles, arranged the fluted pleats of her apricot silk dress, as if she were posing for a fashion magazine layout.

At least that was the way she impressed Leigh, who was honest enough with herself, however, to admit that she might simply be intimidated by the *signora*'s rather overwhelming beauty. She was the epitome of luscious Italian womanhood: tall and svelte, yet with generous curves in all the right places, and she had big, dark-fringed brown eyes that were undeniably lovely, although they did seem to convey a rather cool haughtiness. Or perhaps they only seemed to, because her flashing smiles never really disturbed the smooth perfection of her face. But she was beautiful nonetheless, beautiful enough, in fact, to make Leigh begin to feel as if she were still in one of those awful caftans and looking every bit as dumpy as she had yesterday. And it didn't help matters at all to realize Marc could certainly have fallen in love with such an exquisite creature as Sophia. That realization gave some credibility to Angelica's claim that he was her father, plus the fact that she did resemble him. But no, Leigh thought, she couldn't allow herself to think that way. He had denied that he was Angelica's father and she wanted so much to believe him that she pushed her doubts far back in her mind and, instead, concentrated on the girl's reaction to her mother.

She was a different child, bubbly rather than sullen, and more animated than Leigh had ever imagined she could be. Barely taking the time to pause for breath, she was telling Sophia everything that had happened to her in the four weeks since they had seen each other. But as she began to relate in great detail what her paternal grandparents had written in a letter to her, Sophia heaved a silent sigh and glanced at Leigh.

"Is it not time for Angelica's afternoon rest?" she asked coolly, interrupting her daughter's excited chatter. "It is nearly two o'clock."

Leigh's eyes darted to the child's crestfallen expression, and she wondered at the mother's lack of sensitivity. Even she, a mere companion, had thought that Angelica could miss her nap today since it was such a special occasion.

"Oh, Mama, no," the girl protested, her voice husky and her chin wobbling. "I have not seen you in such a long time, and there is so much I want to tell you."

"We will have plenty of time to chat later," Sophia said with a blithe wave of her hand. Then suddenly the bored expression on her face was wiped away, as if by magic, to be replaced by a sultry smile of welcome. It was Marc who was the catalyst for the transformation, and Sophia held out her hands beckoningly as he strode out through the open French doors from the sitting room onto the piazza. "Darling Marc," she whispered seductively, pulling him down to her as he took her hands. Her lips pressed against his lean tanned cheek, then parted with a breathless, imcomprehensible murmur as they moved over to linger against his. "I cannot tell you how much it pleases me to see you again."

"You don't need to tell him, or anyone else, that," Leigh thought disgustedly, looking away from the suspiciously intimate display of affection. It was obvious Sophia was far more interested in Marc as an attractive man than as a brother-in-law, and judging by the way he allowed her to cling to his hands, he apparently did not object. Unable to prevent herself, Leigh glanced their way again, then wished she hadn't, as she found Marc watching her, a somewhat sardonic smile tugging at the corners of his mouth. Hating herself for the blush that crept hotly into her cheeks, she looked away again hastily, turning her attention to the girl in the wheelchair, who was still gazing at her mother adoringly.

"How are you, Sophia?" Marc asked after a moment of silence. "What made you tear yourself away from your friends on the French Riviera? Surely not a sense of maternal responsibility?"

Leigh's eyes darted to his face as he uttered those words, but since he was smiling rather indulgently down at his sister-in-law, he had apparently only been teasing. Sophia was accepting his comment with a coy laugh from down deep in her throat.

"Darling, you know me well, do you not?" she countered without a hint of apology. "I do my damnedest to forget my maternal responsibilities. I am far too young to have a thirteen-year-old child anyway. Angelica and I are more like sisters, *si, bambina?*"

"Si, Mama," the girl answered quickly, eager to

share any sort of relationship with her mother. "We are like sisters but—but I will never be as beautiful as you are."

"How sweet you are to say that," Sophia said, without so much as a halfhearted attempt to deny her daughter's words. And as she unnecessarily smoothed her gleaming cap of black hair, she suddenly frowned again as Marcus reassured the child for her.

"You will be a beauty someday, Angelica," he said kindly, pulling his hands from Sophia's grasp to cup his niece's chin. "In a few more years, the boys will be beating a path to your door. You may even surpass your Mother. You should have seen her when she was your age—she was too tall and too skinny and her mouth was far too big. *And* she was ridiculously clumsy."

"Really, Marcus, you make me sound as if I were a walking disaster," Sophia muttered petulantly, stiffening in her chair. "I was not all that bad, surely."

Marc's eyes gleamed rather wickedly. "Perhaps we should ask your parents to send Angelica some photographs of you when you were thirteen. In fact, I may just phone them tonight and ask them to."

"Then you will be wasting your time if you do," Sophia retorted, her eyes mirroring her displeasure at the conversation. "I destroyed all the old photographs of me years ago."

"Oh, I wish you had not, Mama," Angelica said sadly. "Now I will never believe you were ever as ugly as I am."

"But you aren't ugly at all," Leigh felt compelled to contribute. She grinned wryly, reminiscently. "You're very beautiful compared to what I looked like when I was thirteen. I was skinny as a rail and had so many freckles on my face that the boys called me Huckleberry Finn."

Though Angelica and Marc laughed at her self-description, Sophia only managed to force a tight little smile that faded almost instantaneously. Then she made a great show of glancing at her gold, diamond-studded wristwatch.

"Oh dear, I am afraid you *must* go up to your room for your rest now, *bambina mia,*" she announced with no sign of genuine regret. And when Angelica began to protest, Sophia's lips closed tightly, and with this impatient expression on her face she no longer looked so youthful and dewy-fresh. She shook a warning finger at her daughter. "If you are going to be difficult when I come visit you, *bambina,* then perhaps I should not come so often."

You call once every four weeks often? Leigh wanted to ask sarcastically and perhaps some of her disapproval was showing in her face because she looked up and found Marc watching her. His green eyes narrowed, almost as if issuing a challenge, which caused her heart to begin beating erratically. She had no desire to get involved in another confrontation with him, especially one concerning Sophia. Besides, the woman's actions were none of her business anyway, as he would undoubtedly tell her if she dared interfere.

Her mother's threat had effectively silenced Angelica's protests anyway. Pitifully eager to please, she gestured nervously for Leigh to get up and come get her. "I am tired, *signorina,*" she said meekly. "Please, take me up to my room." Then she cast a hopeful look in her mother's direction. "I will see you at dinner though, will I not, Mama?"

"We shall see, *bambina,*" Sophia answered with a careless, noncommittal shrug of her silk-covered shoulders. Then she prodded the girls along with a limp wave of her hand. "Go on now. Take your nap and let me have Marc to myself. I have so many things to tell him."

Suddenly, Leigh felt a nearly overwhelming contempt for the glamorous Sophia. A beauty she might be, but as a mother she was a dismal failure. And even as Marcus ruffled his niece's hair comfortingly as Leigh pushed the wheelchair past him, she could not help but be disappointed in him too, because there was a chance he could be in love with a woman as shallow as Sophia.

As the week passed, Leigh's indignation grew. Angelica began every day waiting, hoping her mother would spend some time with her. But every day, Sophia slept until noon, then rushed off for a late lunch in the town of Capri, followed by an afternoon of extravagant spending in the fashionable shops there. By the end of each day, Angelica was slumping disappointedly in her wheelchair staring at her hands, and nothing Leigh tried to do to rouse her from her lethargy helped in the slightest.

Sometimes, Sophia deigned to stop a moment when she returned from shopping to say a quick hello to her daughter, and during those rare times, Leigh felt an almost overpowering desire to chastise her soundly. She acted more like a silly schoolgirl than a woman, and in her Leigh saw very strong similarities to Stefano. Both were no more mature than spoiled children, but of the two of them, Sophia was the more frustrating individual. Even though she had given birth to Angelica at a very young age, she was still the girl's mother and owed her at least a little attention.

All of Sophia's attention, however, went to her shopping forays, or, in the evenings, to Marc. Though he never allowed anyone to disturb his work during the day, his nights were free. So every evening, after dinner, Sophia staked her claim to him and, with silent barbed glances, warned both Angelica and Leigh not to make nuisances of themselves.

As far as Leigh was concerned, she would have preferred retiring to her room and leaving Marc and Sophia alone, but Angelica would not give up so easily. She stayed as close as possible to her mother when everyone went into the salon for coffee after dinner. To his credit, Marc did try to include both her and Leigh in all conversations, but somehow Sophia managed to change the subject to some topic that effectively excluded them. After a while, even Angelica would realize how futile it was to remain in the salon, and in a sad little voice that made Leigh ache with compassion for her, she would ask to be taken up to her room.

A wrought-iron elevator, installed in the villa's main hall by the previous owner, made it simple to get Angelica up to the second floor. It was one of those ancient conveyances that required more than a mere push of the button, and usually Angelica enjoyed manning the controls herself, but on Thursday night she made no move to do so.

"The door is closed so we're ready to go, operator," Leigh prompted, hoping to elicit at least a wan smile. "Come on, Angie. You're the pro at running this thing. When I try, we tend to ascend in quick bumps and stop with a lurch—remember?"

"I will let you operate the controls tonight anyway," the child muttered despondently. "I do not want to do it, *signorina.*"

"All right, it's your neck," Leigh teased, stepping forward to the levers, then glancing back over her shoulder. "You know, instead of calling me that so formal *signorina,* you could start calling me by my first name. I wouldn't mind at all."

"All right—Leigh." Lifting her chin from off her chest, Angelica chewed her lower lip then blurted out: "Will you tell me something, *signo*—Leigh? Does your mother like you?"

"Well, I'm sure she has her moments when she's not exactly wild about me but—but yes, for the most part, I think she likes me," Leigh answered honestly, knowing a lie would never be believed anyway. Angelica was too nonperceptive a child to be taken in—even by an attempt to give her comfort. All Leigh could do was offer a sympathetic ear. "Why don't you tell me why you asked me that question?"

"You know why," Angelica whispered, a sudden sob escaping her. Another followed, then another, and when the elevator stopped upstairs, Leigh pushed the wheelchair quickly down the hall to the girl's room.

"Cry it all out," she whispered consolingly, handing the child several tissues. "You know, in the two weeks I've been here, I've never seen you cry once—so I think it's about time you do a good job of it."

"I—I do not like to—to cry, though," Angelica said haltingly. "It—it always irritates M-Mama so much when I do."

"Well, I'm sure your mama cries too," Leigh declared, managing not to sound too caustic. "All women cry, honey. And it usually does them good. It may be one of the reasons they generally live longer than men, who think they have to keep up a brave front all the time."

"But I have never seen M-Mama cry." Angelica's sobs began anew. "Oh, why can I not be just the way she is? So beautiful and carefree? If I were, she might like me."

"I'm sure she likes you just the way you are. She simply may be one of those people who can't show their feelings easily."

"You think so?" Angelica asked urgently, her eyes lighting up as she eagerly clung to even that vague hope. "You really think she does like me?"

"How could she not?" Leigh countered with a grin. "When you try you can be a very sweet girl, you know."

Ducking her head, Angelica muttered, "I was not very sweet to you when you first came here. I am very sorry."

"Apology accepted," Leigh said lightly, going to take the girl's soft, yellow nightgown from a dresser drawer. "Now, you put this on and go brush your teeth, then I'll help you into bed."

Though Angelica nodded and began unbuttoning her

blouse, she looked up after a moment. "Would you—Could you stay with me until—until I go to sleep? Please, just this one time? I know it is very silly and childish but—"

"It isn't silly at all and of course I'll stay," Leigh said gently and when she was rewarded with a tremulous little smile of gratitude, she clenched her fists impotently at her sides. This child was so transparently lonely it was truly pathetic, and she needed much more than the affection and sympathy of a paid companion. She needed a parent. A determined glint suddenly illuminated Leigh's blue eyes. Even if she lost her job here for interfering, tomorrow she had to speak to Marc about Angelica's depression. Something had to be done for her soon, and whether or not Sophia wanted the responsibility, she was really the only person who could make her daughter feel loved.

Talking to Marc Saturday proved to be no easy accomplishment, however. All morning he was locked away in his darkroom where, of course, Leigh did not dare disturb him. Then immediately after lunch, a crowd of Sophia's friends descended on the villa, to lounge lazily by the pool or stroll idly through the gardens. Never in her life had Leigh seen so many blase people grouped all together in one place. In many ways they looked like clones of one another. Deeply tanned, fashionably gaunt and expensively dressed, they all wore the same utterly bored expressions on their smooth facile faces. People who assumed that pose of ennui had always irritated Leigh immensely, but after getting Angelica settled for her afternoon rest, she went back downstairs among them anyway, to search for Marc.

He seemed to have vanished. After threading through the crowd around the portable bar on the piazza and enduring the blatantly appraising stares of the male guests, Leigh sought refuge in the garden only to narrowly escape being cornered by a curly-haired middle-aged man with an unpleasantly dissolute face. She decided the house was the safest place to be, and after sneaking in through the kitchen she hurried to Marc's study. The door was slightly ajar, but when she started to knock the sound of Sophia's angry voice stopped her.

"I do have a life of my own, Marc," she was saying impatiently. "You seem to be forgetting that."

"And you seem to be forgetting you're also a mother," he countered calmly. "Of course, you've never taken that responsibility very seriously, have you?"

A heavy, dramatic sigh was followed by the sound of movement and when Sophia spoke again, her voice was low and huskily beseeching. "I have done my best for Angelica. You know that, don't you, Marc? But I am just not the motherly type. I am the first to admit it."

"And I suppose you think admitting it makes everything all right?" he retorted impatiently. "If you tell the world you weren't meant to be a mother, then you no longer have to try to be one—is that it? If that is your idea of the way things work then you're very much mistaken. No matter what you say or do, you are still Angelica's mother and she needs you. Do you realize you've ignored her all week? And after promising to spend today with her, instead you invite all these idiot friends of yours here and disappoint her again."

"I simply forgot I had promised her," Sophia whined. "Is that such a terrible crime?"

"Oh for God's sake!" Marc exploded, then, after a moment, apparently relented somewhat. "Children can be very fragile, especially a child like Angelica. Quite frankly, I don't know how many more broken promises she can stand. Why is it so difficult for you to simply spend some time with her?"

"It is that horrid wheelchair!" Sophia exclaimed, angry again. "I feel faint every time I see her in it! You know how squeamish I am about any kind of sickness. I cannot bear to be around people who are ill, either physically or mentally."

"Then you're just going to have to force yourself to bear it, because you are going to spend some time with Angelica before you leave here—and if I have to tie you down somewhere to make you do it, I will."

"But I—I cannot do that!"

"You can sure as hell give it a try," he answered harshly. "And by God, this time you're going to."

"Marc, darling, please," Sophia began in her silliest juvenile whine. "I—"

"Enough. I've made up my mind, Sophia," he interrupted coolly. "Now you had better be getting back to your guests. And you can tell them the party's over no later than midnight tonight. After that, I want every one of them out of here."

With a cry of rage, Sophia rushed to the door, flinging it open before Leigh could slip away. "Get out of my way, *signorina!*" the older woman ordered rudely, tossing her head as she marched down the hall out of sight.

Suddenly, as Leigh watched her disappear, a relieved smile played upon her lips. But the smile faded instantaneously and she gasped suddenly as Marc came to the door. He gripped her wrist roughly, jerking her without gentleness into the study and closed the door.

"Did you want to talk to me about something?" he asked, his eyes a frosty green as they surveyed the white gauze sundress she wore. "Or do you make a habit of eavesdropping?"

"Of course not!" Leigh glared up at him, then gestured uncertainly. "Well, I guess I was eavesdropping just now—but only because you were discussing the very thing I'd come to see you about."

A sudden grin gentled his rugged features.

"You're an honest little thing, aren't you? So, you came to talk to me about Angelica?"

Leigh nodded, fighting the urge to reach up and

touch light fingertips against the faint lines that deepened around his eyes as he smiled.

"Yes, I came about Angelica," she said at last. "I'm very concerned about her and—well, I suppose it was presumptuous of me but I was going to ask you to speak to Signora Cavalli about spending more time with her. But—"

"But when you heard me ordering her to do just that, you decided to just stand outside the door and listen."

"I apologize for that."

"You're forgiven, then. At least you show some interest in my niece, and I've been meaning to tell you how much I appreciate it."

"It's what you pay me for, isn't it?"

"No, you can't pay people to care about each other," he said softly, taking a step forward, diminishing the distance between them. "I pay you to be with Angelica, to help her get around, and to simply be there so she won't be too lonely but the fact that you care about her has nothing to do with the money I pay you—and you know that very well, Leigh. You *give* her your affection now, even though you didn't really like her much when you first arrived here."

"I know her better now, so I like her."

"Oh, and do you always like people after you get to know them?"

"Well, no, I didn't say that," she murmured, wondering at his mysterious tone. "Sometimes I like people *until* I get to know them better, then I don't like them."

"And in which category do I fit?" he asked wryly, his dark green eyes holding hers in a teasing gaze. "Would you care to tell me?"

Leigh shook her head.

"I—I haven't made up my mind about you yet. I guess I don't know you well enough."

Laughing softly, Marc cupped her chin in one hand.

"A very diplomatic answer, Miss Sheridan," he said with only a trace of mockery. Then, as his thumb brushed slowly along her high cheekbone, his eyes narrowed and he turned her head first to one side, then the other. "Umm, interesting," he murmured finally. "Did you know you have very unusual skin? It's the exact color of pale honey, and the texture is perfect. You may be just what I've been looking for."

"Looking for?" Leigh said weakly, wishing his thumb didn't create such havoc with her senses. "I—I don't know what you mean."

"I mean I still want to photograph you. Remember, I mentioned it before? Now, I have something specific in mind. A friend of mine owns a cosmetic firm and, though I don't ever get involved in advertising, he asked me to find a model with exquisite skin and take some shots of her down amongst the camellia shrubs in the garden. That's the name of his newest line of skin-care products, *Camellia.* Are you interested in being the *Camellia* girl, Miss Sheridan?"

"Me?" she exclaimed softly. "You really think I might do?"

"You will do—I've decided," he announced. "I had thought of using Sophia but you're a much better choice. So, tomorrow afternoon at one, meet me in the garden by the camellias. The light will be right then. Okay?"

"But I've never posed for—"

"And you won't pose tomorrow either. I'll try to get some natural, impromptu shots."

"Wh—What should I wear though? I'm afraid I don't have anything fancy."

Marc grinned again.

"You don't need anything fancy. What you're wearing right now will be fine, as a matter of fact." He released her chin slowly, trailing his fingers along the smooth line of her jaw, but when she moistened her suddenly dry lips with the tip of her tongue his hand dropped and he moved away. "I don't mean to be rude, Miss Sheridan, but I'm behind on my work so—"

"Of course, I want to check in on Angelica anyway," she said hastily, making a beeline for the door where she paused only a second. "Tomorrow afternoon then."

"Promptly at one or we'll lose the best light," was his parting reminder.

Nodding, Leigh slipped out into the hall where she leaned for a moment against the cool wall. What had she gotten herself into this time? All her life, she had looked dreadful in photographs, too stiff and self-conscious with her pained little smiles. And knowing Marc was behind the camera tomorrow, watching her every move, she would be lucky if she didn't die of camera shyness. At the very best, she was sure she would look like some kind of zombie.

Sunday afternoon, after lunch, Leigh ran a brush through her hair until it was shining and when she had checked her appearance in the full-length mirror in her room, she hurried downstairs, out into the sunshine. Angelica was with Signora Rossetti, learning to monogram handkerchiefs. Though it was only twenty till one, Leigh could not sit still. She was ridiculously nervous about the coming photograph session and it crossed her mind frequently to just tell Marc she couldn't go through with it. Yet, she was afraid to do that too. He probably wouldn't appreciate her backing out at the last minute.

Trying to ease some of her tension, she walked at a brisk pace through the rose gardens, stopping occasionally to inhale the sweet fragrance of plentiful blooms. It was under one of the rose bushes that she discovered the kitten. Mottled gray, and rather bedraggled, he shrank back against the woody base of the sprawling bush. But when Leigh reached her hand in slowly to him, rubbing her fingers together gently, he became more courageous.

"Are you a lost cat?" she said quietly as he brushed

his whiskers against her hand. "You don't look old enough to leave your mama yet, so where is she?"

The kitten, of course, provided no answers to her questions, but when he began to purr contentedly as she stroked his soft fur he won her over completely. She started playing with him, trailing a long twig across the flagstone walkway so he could chase it. And she was so caught up in their game that she nearly forgot to check the time. When she finally glanced at her watch it was three until one.

"Oh glory, he'll probably kill me if I'm late," she told the kitten, scooping him up gently in her arms, then rushing away to the opposite side of the grounds where the camellias grew.

Though Marc didn't kill her, he did give her a rather impatient look as she half ran into the secluded bower the camellia shrubs made, the kitten trying to climb up on her shoulder.

"The light filtering through those trees is fading fast, Miss Sheridan," he announced brusquely. "So if you'll stop playing *Wild Kingdom* and put down that cat, I'd like to get started shooting."

"Yes *sir,*" she responded, regretting the hint of sarcasm in her voice almost immediately as he glowered at her. Obviously he took his business very seriously, she thought, as she put the kitten down out of camera range. Turning back to Marc, she smoothed first her hair, then the skirt of her white dress with shaky fingers. "Wh—Where should I stand?"

He glanced up from the camera he was adjusting on a tripod. "We'll position you exactly in a minute. Go ahead and take your clothes off first," he said, as calmly as if he had told her to say cheese.

Leigh could almost feel the blood draining from her face, and as her legs weakened, she took a staggered step backward. *Take your clothes off first.* That was what he had said! For a few breathless moments, she was utterly speechless but she finally managed to find her voice.

"B—But I—I—but you—you didn't say anything about—."

"What are you babbling about, Leigh?" Marc asked rather irritably. But apparently when he glanced up, she was looking even greener than she felt. Mumbling beneath his breath, he strode quickly to her and grasped her shoulders in iron-hard hands. "For God's sake, don't faint. It was only a joke. You don't have to take off your clothes. Unless, of course, you really want to. I certainly won't object."

The blood rushed back fast and hot to her cheeks. "What—What do you mean it was only a joke?" she muttered through clenched teeth. "You mean you—you just said that to embarrass me?"

"You're acting very flustered for an experienced young woman of twenty-five," he answered softly, encircling her neck with caressing hands. "But you're not very experienced, are you? It's fairly obvious this Stefano of yours is your first lover."

"Stefano isn't—"

"And it's even more obvious that you're not twenty-five, so exactly how old are you?" His fingers tangled in the thick silky hair on her nape imprisoning her with the promise that any movement she made would be painful. "How old, Leigh? The truth this time, all right?"

She was sorely tempted for a moment not to answer him, but judging by the implacable set of his jaw, he wouldn't let her go until she did.

"Twenty-one. I'm twenty-one," she admitted begrudgingly. "Now, are you satisfied?"

"Can I be sure you won't tell me you're eighteen the next time I ask?" he countered. "I'd like some assurances that you're telling the truth for once."

"You'll just have to trust me," she snapped at him,

trying to pull away and wincing as his fingers tightened in her hair. "Let me go! You've had enough fun at my expense! I must say you bait your traps imaginatively—pictures to advertise some mythical skin care product. Very original, Mr. Cavalli."

"It's Marc, remember? I think we went way beyond the Mr. Cavalli stage the other night in your room, don't you?" Without allowing her to answer, he gripped her shoulders again to push her gently back near a camellia shrub, heavy with pure white blooms. "Now, stay right in this general area and touch the flowers occasionally. Do anything. Just pay no attention to me while I'm shooting and we'll get some very nice shots for my friend, I'm sure."

"But—"

"The ad campaign for *Camellia* products isn't mythical, I assure you," he said, backing away. "Now just relax and act natural."

Amazingly, she did relax, eventually almost forgetting the camera, and after a while, when he allowed her to play with the kitten, she felt much less self-conscious. At least, she was no longer the only object of attention. Occasionally, Marc stopped shooting to move her to different places, following the light, he explained, but the last time he came he only took the kitten from her arms. As he put the cat down gently on the ground and she noticed the disturbing rippling of muscles in his back, outlined against the thin knit fabric of his black polo shirt, she felt an astonishingly intense desire to touch him.

"Wh—Where should I stand this time?" she murmured instead.

"Right here is fine," he answered, straightening and spanning her narrow waist before she could react. "I've finished shooting."

"Then let me go," she demanded icily, pushing futilely at his chest. "I'd like to go to my room."

"Are you sure you won't change your mind and take

your clothes off for me after all?" he whispered provocatively into her ear. "Umm, Leigh?"

Before she could begin to utter an indignant retort, he was gently tracing the shape of her lips, his thumb teasing their fullness until they parted breathlessly. Then he tugged her mouth open slightly and lowered his own, whispering her name.

An aching thrill pulsated through her, sending a shiver of delight along her spine, and suddenly she wanted nothing more than to touch him, to feel his smooth warm skin beneath her hands. Almost of their own volition, her fingers slid up over his chest to begin a shaky exploration of his lean face.

With a soft groan, he crushed her to him, devouring her lips until she was clinging to him, supple, warm and infinitely yielding in his arms. And when he finally released her mouth from the savage onslaught of his, it was to draw her into the secluded cul-de-sac formed by the camellia shrubs. Taking acquiescence for granted, he lowered himself to the petal-covered ground, his strong hand squeezing hers, as he pulled her down to lie beside him. He turned her toward him, and as their bodies touched, a searing passion surged between them and Leigh opened her mouth to the seeking lips that covered hers, responding with an urgency that nearly equalled his.

With a muffled exclamation, he bore her down onto the velvety petals, his mouth hard and possessive as he teased her soft lips with gentle nips of strong white teeth. She shuddered as the rough surface of the tip of his tongue tasted the minty sweetness of her own. Her fingers tangled in his dark, thick hair, urging a rougher taking of her mouth, and as his lips twisted the tender fullness of hers, she strained against him, trying to ease the sudden, aching emptiness that dragged at her lower limbs.

As one heavy, muscular leg covered both hers, the evidence of his desire throbbed warm and iron-hard against her slender thigh. When he released her mouth, her eyes flickered open to gaze up wonderingly into the green fire of his.

"How do you manage to look so innocent?" he muttered, his voice deep and appealing with throaty huskiness. "Hasn't your Stefano ever made you feel this way? Hasn't anyone?"

As she closed her eyes on the nearly mesmerizing, triumphant flare of desire in his, strangely shaking fingers eased the straps of her dress from her shoulders. "*Marc,*" she sighed as his breath cooled the warm hollow between her breasts. His large hand spread open on her abdomen, hard and warm through the thin gauze dress, and when he pressed his palm against her hipbone, his fingers curved possessively—gentle, yet conveying a dizzying message. Until that moment, Leigh had never completely understood a man's innate power over a woman, the sheer superior physical strength that meant he could take what he wanted, should she choose not to give it freely. A flicker of fear warred with the hot, intense needs his touch evoked in her. His hands wandered over her, then, as his fingertips slipped beneath her skirt to trail fire along the sensitive skin of her inner thighs just above her knees, she tensed.

"Relax," he coaxed, his lips playing over hers. "Let me take your clothes off, Leigh. I need to see the sunlight dancing over every inch of that delectable skin of yours."

His words restored reason with a jolt, and she pulled free, scurrying to stand on ridiculously weak legs. "You'll have to find somebody else to play 'Adam and Eve in the garden' with you, Mr. Cavalli," she informed him, her voice embarrassingly unsteady. "Because I'm not about to take my clothes off."

"Scared, aren't you?" he retorted, smiling rather wickedly as he also rose to his feet. "You're afraid I might want to do much more than just look at you."

Furious with herself for blushing hotly, Leigh spun around on one heel and marched back toward the villa.

"Little coward," he called after her. "*Bambina.*"

Though she could hear him laughing softly behind her, she thrust out her chin and went on—relieved that he believed she only feared him. But that wasn't precisely true. Warring with the fear was a far more disconcerting reaction—the deepening desire she was beginning to feel: to experience what would undoubtedly happen if she ever did take her clothes off for him.

Chapter Six

Angelica and the kitten fell in love at first sight. Though Leigh had been his rescuer and the provider of saucers of warm milk, the cat showed a definite preference for the younger girl's company. There seemed to be the instant rapport between them that children and animals often have, and before Leigh knew it, she was the odd man out—not that she minded. At least when Angelica was holding the kitten she seemed relatively happy, and some of that lost, desolate look left her face.

"What are you going to name your kitten?" Angelica asked late Monday morning, a hint of longing in her voice. "Have you thought of anything yet?"

As Leigh looked up from the button she was sewing on the child's blouse, she grinned.

"How can you call him my kitten? Look at him snuggling up on your lap as if he's found a permanent home. He pays no attention to me when you're around, so maybe you better just name him yourself. He's more yours than mine."

"Really, *signorina?*" Angelica whispered hopefully, her black eyes sparkling. "Would you really give him to me?"

"He isn't mine to give. Cats are independent little creatures. They make up their own minds and this one has definitely decided he wants to belong to you." Leigh smiled at the joyous excitement that illuminated the girl's thin face. "And I bet your uncle wouldn't even mind if you keep the kitten in your room at night."

"Oh, that would be so wonderful. But—" Angelica shook her head sadly. "But Mama would never let me, even if Marcus would. She does not like cats at all."

And cats don't like her either if they have good sense, Leigh thought uncharitably.

"Perhaps I could hide the kitten from her," Angelica suggested rather guiltily. "It would be wrong to do that, I know, but it would be so nice if he could sleep in my room—because I get scared sometimes at night. Do—you?"

Nodding, Leigh blinked back the sudden tears of compassion that sprang to her eyes. "Why don't we decide how to persuade your mother after we talk to your uncle."

"After you talk to me about what?" Marc asked suddenly from just behind them, his rubber-soled shoes making no sound as he came around to stand disturbingly close beside Leigh. Resting one hand on the back of her chair, he eyed both girls suspiciously. "What are you two *young* ladies plotting?" When his deliberate emphasis on the word young brought Leigh's eyes darting up to meet his, he seemed to be laughing at her resentful glare. "Well, speak up. What did you want to talk to me about?"

"Could—could I keep this kitten in my room at night?" Angelica blurted out pleadingly. "Oh, Uncle Marcus, please say yes, *please.* Leigh says he likes me and I just love him. I will take care of him if you let me. He will not be any trouble, I promise."

For a long silent moment, Marc only stared pensively at his niece's upturned face, then, shrugging, he smiled gently. "I see no reason why he can't stay in your room, *piccola,* if that's what will make you happy."

"It is! Oh, it is," Angelica cried joyously, burying her face in the kitten's soft fur. And, when she lifted her head again, she giggled excitedly. "But I still have not thought of a name for him. What do you think it should be, Uncle Marcus?"

Eyeing the cat, Marc stroked his chin as if he were giving the question very serious thought. Then he smiled mischievously. "Are you even sure 'he' is a he? Or could he possibly be a she?"

Angelica looked at Leigh. "Signorina, do you know?"

"Well, no, I—"

"You mean you didn't check?" Marc exclaimed, more than a hint of amusement in his voice. "Weren't you curious?"

"No, I wasn't curious," she retorted, willing herself not to blush as she shrugged: "Whether it was a boy or girl didn't seem to matter."

"It matters to the kitten, *bambina mia.*"

"Don't call me that," Leigh whispered indignantly, as Angelica turned the kitten onto its back on her lap to begin the necessary examination. "I am not a *bambina,* and if I were I most certainly wouldn't be yours."

Leaning down so that his face was very close to hers, he whispered, "But you are my baby now, Leigh. I thought I was getting someone older than twenty-one to be a companion for my niece, but I got you. And now, instead of having one little girl in my house, I have two."

"I am not a—"

"How do you know if it is a boy or a girl?" Angelica interrupted, mercifully. "I cannot tell."

"Take my word for it, *piccola,*" Marc said, straightening. "That kitten is distinctly female. See how nice, quiet and demure she is?—the way girls are supposed to be."

Though Leigh sniffed impatiently, Angelica took him at his word.

"I am glad she is a girl. But what should I name her?"

"Something soft and very pretty," Marc suggested, walking over to stroke the kitten's thick fur. But his eyes never left Leigh. "How about Camellia? What do you think of that as a name, Miss Sheridan?"

"Fine," was her terse answer. And she refused to smile back as he smiled with sudden indulgence at her. He had suggested that name deliberately. Now, every time Angelica called that kitten Leigh would be reminded of yesterday afternoon, as he had known she would be.

"Camellia," Angelica whispered softly. "I like that."

Leigh relaxed suddenly, responding to the unusual happiness in the girl's voice. But, unfortunately, the contentment of the moment was short lived. From the sitting room, Sophia strolled out onto the piazza, cool and elegant in midnight-blue silk lounging pajamas. A look of pure horror, however, replaced the indolent expression on her face when she noticed the kitten sleeping on her daughter's lap.

"For heaven's sake Angelica, get that nasty creature off you at once," she said shrilly. "You never know where it has been."

As his niece's cheeks paled Marc interceded. "Cats are relatively clean animals, Sophia," he said calmly. "So there's no need for you to get all in a dither."

"But Marc darling, they scratch!"

"Oh, my kitten would not scratch me Mama," Angelica protested. "She is much too nice. And her name is Camellia. Isn't she pretty? Leigh gave her to me."

Sophia's anger focused on Leigh immediately. "That was very irresponsible of you, *signorina,*" she said, her words clipped. "Did it not occur to you to ask my permission before giving my daughter a cat?"

"She had my permission, Sophia," Marc interceded once again. "I think it will do Angelica good to have a pet."

With a sigh of pure frustration, Sophia threw up her hands. "All right, all right, if you say she can keep a pet, I suppose she can—as long as the creature stays outside at all times."

"But, Mama—"

"I also told her she could keep Camellia in her room at night," Marc said without apology. "It can't hurt her, Sophia." And when she shuddered visibly, then flounced down onto a vacant chair, he took a seat also, resting his elbows on his knees. "I'm glad you came down here. I wanted to talk to you about some plans I've made for tomorrow."

"Excuse me please," Leigh murmured, getting to her feet hastily. They didn't need her presence for this family discussion. But as she started to slip away quietly, Marc stopped her.

"Sit back down please, Leigh—these plans include you too." When Angelica looked up curiously, he grinned at her. "How would you like to go on an all-day outing tomorrow, *piccola?* With your mother, Miss Sheridan, and me?"

Though the girl squealed with delight, her mother's reaction was far less exuberant.

"Outing, Marcus? What do you mean?"

"I mean we take Angelica out for a day of fun. She's never explored Capri—amazingly enough, she's never even seen the Blue Grotto."

"Neither have I, nor do I ever want to," Sophia said bitingly. "All those sightseer's haunts are so *touriste.*"

"Well, I'd love to see the Blue Grotto and the Green and White and Red, wouldn't you, Angelica?" Leigh spoke up perversely. "I'd hate to leave Capri without seeing them."

"Good. So tomorrow we're all going to act like tourists," Marc said, winking at his niece. "We'll get up bright and early and spend the whole day seeing the sights."

"Bright and early?" Sophia groaned. "Oh darling, you know what a sleepyhead I am early in the morning."

Now, how would he know what she was like in the mornings, Leigh asked herself, but the only logical answer was so disturbing that she swiftly pushed it far to the back of her mind to concentrate instead on what Sophia was saying.

"I will never be able to get out of bed at six in the morning!" she was insisting indignantly. "Such an ungodly hour! But I know what we can do. You, Marc, take Angelica out early then come back for Signorina Sheridan and me early in the afternoon."

"But, Mama, I would like you to spend the whole day with me."

"And she's going to," Marc said firmly, an unmistakable warning in his eyes as he stared at his sister-in-law. "Aren't you, Sophia?"

"I do not like to be ordered about, Marc," she muttered belligerently, ". . . even by you."

"But I'm not ordering you to do anything. You know you really want to spend the day with Angelica. You told me so yourself," he prompted, his body tensed, conveying latent danger. "Now ease the child's mind and tell her the way you really feel about tomorrow—that you're looking forward to seeing Capri with her."

Perhaps Sophia sensed, wisely, that she would be very sorry if she didn't take his hint, because she suddenly forced a bright smile at her daughter. "Of course, *bambina mia,* I am looking forward to being with you. We will have a very nice time."

Though Angelica accepted the lie with near pathetic

eagerness, Leigh hardly noticed. She was too busy wondering if Marc's concern for the girl didn't go past what an uncle would usually feel for a niece. And she was also wondering why Sophia, obstinate, headstrong and selfish as she was, seemed to bow to his wishes where the girl was concerned. It was an inconsistency that Leigh couldn't understand—unless Marc had been lying and Angelica really was his daughter as she claimed. . . .

They visited the Blue Grotto last, after the White, Red, and Green. As their boatman rowed his *barca* in a circular opening in the rock, so low that they were all forced to duck their heads, Leigh closed her eyes. When she opened them again they were gliding across sapphire water surrounded by the black walls of the cavern. Through a huge arch beneath the waterline lay the open sea and sunlight, reflected by the grotto's white sandy bottom sixty feet below. It seemed a magical place. Other *barcas* and their passengers were dark silhouettes against the bright blue surface of the water. Luigi, their boatman, rowed them near the perimeter of the cave above the site where divers had discovered an ancient statue of Poseidon lying on the sandy bottom.

Perhaps it was the near cathedral-like atmosphere that made everyone speak in the softest of whispers—or not speak at all. Leigh could have relaxed in the shimmering peace and quiet indefinitely. Unfortunately, Sophia was soon restless.

"Marc darling, could we please leave this place?" she whispered loudly. "It is so close in here that I feel as if I am suffocating."

"Luigi, *per favore,*" Marc prompted the boatman, who immediately dipped silent oars into the crystalline water and began rowing them out. Beneath a bright blue sky dotted occasionally with the white fluff of a cumulus cloud, Leigh squinted in the sunlight.

"Oh that was so lovely, Uncle Marcus," Angelica said dreamily. "I only wish Camellia could have come with us and seen it too."

"I'm sure Camellia isn't a great appreciator of water—most cats aren't," he said wryly. "So she's probably very happy that we left her home with a saucer of milk."

"Well, I am pleased that she is happy—because I am not," Sophia said sharply. "I am very tired of sitting in this tiny boat. No more grottoes, please—they all look the same to me anyway."

Shrugging, he checked his wristwatch.

"I suppose we could go ahead and have lunch." Reaching forward, he tugged a strand of his niece's hair. "How does that sound to you, *piccola?* Are you hungry yet?"

"Could we have pizza?" she asked hopefully. "At that place where you took me when I first came to stay with you? Ummm, it was so good."

"Pizza! Oh *bambina,* that would be so fattening," Sophia said with a shudder. "You should not get in the habit of eating such things."

"Pizza it shall be," Marc said firmly, daring his sister-in-law with one intense glance to say another word. "I don't think you have to start worrying about your weight yet, Angelica, even if your mother does make counting calories her life's work."

"Oh Marc, you are impossible," Sophia snapped. Subsiding in a huff that lasted until Luigi had deposited them at Marina Grande she started complaining again as Marc carried Angelica to her wheelchair which they had left there earlier. "Really, I do not understand how those men sit in those minute little *barcas* all day long. My legs are so stiff that I am sure I will be limping around for days. Marc, you should have hired a yacht. Then at least we could have stretched our legs."

"Oh Mama, we could not have taken a yacht into the

Blue Grotto," Angelica said, laughing. "It would have filled up the cave, even if we could have gotten through the entrance."

Sophia's brown eyes flashed with anger. "You will not use that sarcastic tone with me ever again," she snapped at her daughter. "I will not tolerate being laughed at by a child."

"But Mama, I was only teasing," Angelica said tremulously, ducking her head. "I would never laugh at you."

As Marc cursed beneath his breath and grasped Sophia's arm, Leigh hastily pushed the wheelchair on toward the parked car. When she glanced back once over her shoulder she did not envy the older woman in the least. Marc was towering over her, gripping her arms, and judging by his stormy expression he was not telling her how lovely she looked in her white slacks and aqua top designed by Emilio Pucci. Whatever he did say to her, though, obviously made quite an impression, because when the two of them reached the car she apologized to her daughter for losing her temper. Even her constant complaining ceased, though she did turn up her nose in distaste when Marc took them to a tiny, unassuming restaurant off one of the narrow back streets in Capri. While he, Angelica, and Leigh shared a puffy, mozzarella-smothered pizza, she nibbled daintily on a green salad.

"Where are we going now?" Angelica asked eagerly after the meal. "Some place special?"

"I think we should go shopping," Sophia said hopefully, but to no avail. When Marc shook his head she pursed her glossed lips in a childish pout.

"We're going to the beautiful isle of Ischia. A launch leaves Marina Grande at one-thirty," he said, consulting his watch. "That's forty-five minutes from now. How would you ladies like to really go tourist and spend that time browsing through the souvenir shops down by the harbor?"

"Oh yes, I would like that!" Angelica said, wriggling excitedly in her chair. "It will be fun, will it not, Leigh?"

"Sounds terrific," Leigh agreed. "Souvenir shops are always crammed with all kinds of interesting things."

"They are no better than junk shops, *signorina,*" Sophia said heatedly. "And I see no point in. . . ." Her words trailed off and a flush crept into her cheeks beneath her toasty tan as Marc gave her a scorching look of warning. "Oh all right, we will visit the souvenir shops, but do not blame me if we are mistaken for tourists."

The shop was indeed a junk lover's paradise. Plaster statues of every saint imaginable covered an entire table above which cheap medallion necklaces hung from hooks in the ceiling. Angelica could hardly contain herself when she spotted a jumbled array of ceramic animals on the floor at the back of the shop, and as she searched for a cat that resembled Camellia, Leigh wandered around until she saw a display of straw tote bags. Most of them sported uneven machine-embroidered maps of the island of Capri—which she thought was a bit much. So she pushed those aside and finally found a few bags that had been left unadorned. Without the glaring decoration, they were simple, attractive, and considering the inexpensive price, reasonably well made.

"Find something you like, Miss Sheridan?" Marc asked suddenly, so close to her ear that his warm breath stirred a wispy tendril of her hair. "Are you going to buy that bag?"

"Well, I—uh—it would make a very nice beach bag but—but—"

"But you neglected to bring any money with you," he finished observantly. "So I'll buy it for you—plus a pair of these straw sandals to go with it."

"Oh but I couldn't let you do—"

"You have a very tiny foot, don't you?" he said, ignoring her protests as he searched through the paired sandals that were dumped all together in a tall basket. "Ah, here we go. These look small enough."

Before Leigh could react, he knelt down in front of her, cupping her ankle in one large, warm hand while removing her leather sandal with the other. Then he slipped the straw one on her foot and looked up at her, lifting his dark brows questioningly.

"It fits perfectly," she murmured, more than a little disconcerted by his solicitous attitude. "Th—They would be nice to wear on the beach."

"Then we'll buy them, and of course the bag too," he said, replacing her leather sandal, then glancing back up at her. "And no arguments."

"I'll repay you as soon as we return to the villa."

"No you won't. Consider them gifts."

"But—"

"Hush, *bambina mia,*" he whispered. His fingers trailed a burning path over the calf of her slender leg up to the smooth skin of her thigh just above her knee as his darkening green eyes held her gaze. "Don't be so obstinate, Leigh. Let me give them to you—I want to. All right?"

She nodded, far too breathless to speak, and as she gazed down at him she felt the craziest urge to tangle her fingers in his dark thick hair. Luckily, before she could succumb to such an insane desire, Angelica wheeled down the aisle toward them and Marc stood to smile at her. Perched on her lap was a two-foot high ceramic cat, mottled gray like her kitten with huge green glass eyes.

"She is just like Camellia. Imagine that—I found one just like Camellia," she said happily, a rather wistful look in her big black eyes. "Uncle Marcus, could I—would you—she is not very costly. Would you—"

"I will buy her for you, yes," he said, then leaned down to add in a whisper, "And go find yourself something else, too—something that will show people that you've explored Capri like a real tourist."

Giggling, she handed over the cat into his keeping and rolled away, adroitly dodging stacks of merchandise that sat in the aisle. Just as she turned out of their sight her mother approached them from behind.

"Do you think we could leave soon, Marc darling?" she asked petulantly. "This untidy place is beginning to give me a headache."

Turning to face her, the cat cradled in his arms, he smiled teasingly.

"What? You mean you haven't found anything you'd like to buy?"

"Hardly," she answered stiffly, turning her nose up again. Then her eyes widened and she grimaced when she noticed the ceramic cat.

"What is that horror you're holding, darling? Surely you're not thinking of purchasing that—that object?"

He was unperturbed by her derogatory tone.

"I certainly am going to buy this. Angelica wants it because it looks like Camellia."

"Camellia?"

"Her new kitten, Sophia," he explained patiently. "Remember? Yesterday she told you she'd named her kitten Camellia."

"Oh yes, she did. Now I recall," Sophia said with a careless wave of her hand. "But still darling, that thing you are holding is—"

"Uncle Marcus, look," Angelica called out behind him. "I found something." She had found something all right—a floppy garish blue hat with the word Capri emblazoned in scarlet letters across the crown.

Her mother gasped as Angelica plopped it down squarely on her head. "Take that ridiculous thing off at once," she commanded haughtily. "I have never ever seen anything so ugly."

"It is pretty tacky, isn't it?" Marc agreed with a grin and a wink at his niece. "But I think it's perfect. Now everyone will know you've been to Capri. We'll buy it."

"*Marc!* You cannot—"

"It's fifteen after one," he interrupted calmly. "We better make our purchases and get down to the quay." Digging into his trouser pocket, he brought forth some *lire* notes which he handed to Angelica. "You and your mother go pay for your things, *piccola,* while I help Leigh decide whether or not she wants to buy the placemats she's been eyeing."

"Anything to escape this drab place," Sophia muttered, shuddering again at her daughter's hat as they negotiated the cluttered aisle.

"Well Leigh, how many placemats do you want?" Marc asked after the other two had left. "Ten, twelve?"

"Oh no, eight would be plenty." She gestured indecisively. "I want them for my mother but—but I hate to ask you to buy me anything else—though of course I would pay you back right away."

"Allow me to buy a gift for your mother too," he said, scooping up ten of the straw placemats along with the sandals and the beach bag. "Now come, if we don't hurry we're going to miss the launch to Ischia."

Because the shopkeeper was busy with another customer, Marc sent Sophia and Angelica down to the pier to board the launch, assuring them that he and Leigh would follow in a moment. The shopkeeper, however, didn't cooperate. He was happily dickering with a French couple over the price of three woven baskets. Several minutes dragged by and Leigh began to worry.

"Maybe we should just forget about buying these things and go to the pier," she suggested finally. "We'll miss the boat if we don't hurry."

"Nonsense," Marc said, smiling down at her. "You want these things so we're buying them. Don't worry about the boat."

After they finally finished in the shop and were back outside, Leigh started to rush down the street.

"You shouldn't run in this heat," Marc said firmly,

catching her arm so that she had to slow down to match his leisurely pace. And when she looked up at him in obvious confusion, he smiled almost indulgently.

They were too late. When they reached the pier the launch to Ischia was moving out to open sea, and Sophia was standing astern at the railing, glaring back at them. Only the topmost part of Angelica's head was visible above the rail.

"Oh, we've missed it!" Leigh exclaimed. "What can we do?"

"Wave," Marc replied laconically, lifting his own hand to do just that. "Ah, alone at last," he murmured after a moment and when Leigh's startled eyes darted to his face, he added: "Angelica and Sophia, I mean. They need some time together with no one else around."

"You missed the launch deliberately, didn't you? You meant for this to happen." Leigh shook her head at him. "But will Signora Cavalli be able to handle Angelica's chair by herself?"

"She'll have to, won't she, until they can catch the next launch back here at four-thirty?" Marc stared out to sea at the launch, his eyes narrowed and thoughtful. "It'll do Sophia good to be totally responsible for Angelica for once. Placed in the position where she has to take care of her. I'm sure she'll do it quite capably. She's not an unintelligent woman—just confused I think."

As he sighed Leigh searched his face, wondering if he was wishing Sophia had not been so confused that she married the wrong brother fourteen years ago. Did he wish she had married him instead? But his expression was completely unreadable, and as she watched him he finally became aware of her appraisal.

One large hand lightly gripped her elbow and he turned her around, guiding her back to his gray Mercedes.

"I've also made some plans for *our* afternoon," he

announced mysteriously as he opened the car door and she got in. And before she could voice her question, he had closed the door again and come around to slide in beneath the steering wheel. As he turned the key in the ignition and the engine roared to life he smiled over at her. "Ready, Miss Sheridan?"

"I—I don't know," she answered haltingly, ridiculously nervous. "Wh—what kind of plans have you made?"

"You ask that as if you don't quite trust me."

"I'm not sure I do," she replied candidly. "Should I?"

"I'm not all that sure myself," he said disturbingly, reaching out to brush the back of his hand against her cheek. "Maybe we'll both find out if you should this afternoon though."

There was a near-promise in his words that set her pulse racing, although he was no longer touching her and had turned his attention to the road that led through Capri.

"Where—where are you taking me, really?" she asked, stilling her trembling hands by clutching them together in her lap. What was it about this man that made her feel she was always walking on the edge of a precipice? Stefano, nor any other man she had ever known, had not affected her the way Marc did. Actually, most men she had met seemed very unexciting, and not one of them had ever really disturbed her emotionally. But Marc was different. He definitely disturbed her, emotionally and physically. Though she knew she was getting too involved with him, she felt herself being as inexorably drawn to him as a moth is drawn to flame. It didn't matter that she told herself repeatedly that she shouldn't let the emotions he aroused overcome her common sense. All she could do was to keep reminding herself that he was too sophisticated for her—that he had affairs with Hollywood starlets and perhaps even with his own sister-in-law.

She herself might seem attractive to him now, but the attraction was purely physical. It would fade quickly, especially if she were to allow an intimate relationship to develop. When that ended he would walk away unscathed while she would never be the same. Eyeing him warily, she persisted, "I asked where you're taking me. I—I'd like to know."

"Don't be so impatient, *bambina mia,*" he said, a hint of laughter in his voice. "You'll know soon enough where we're going and what we're going to do."

He took her to the top of Monte Tiberio to view the ruins of the Villa Jovis, one of the twelve palatial estates the Emperor Tiberius had built on the island.

"He loved it here, obviously," Marc commented, taking Leigh's hand as they walked beneath crumbling stone arches. "In fact he ruled from here the last ten years of his life, refusing to return to Rome. Of course he could have been reluctant to leave the life he had here. Supposedly it was one long orgy—though historians tend to discount that legend now."

"I wonder what the real truth is," Leigh said musingly, looking around, trying to imagine what the villa looked like nearly two thousand years ago. What kind of people had the Romans truly been—the women in their softly draped garments gathered beneath their breasts and the men whose short togas had not detracted in the least from their masculinity? Had they only been interested in sensual pleasures, or had stories about a few of them made them all seem hedonistic? It was an enticing mystery, and she looked up at Marc curiously. "Don't you wonder what they were really like, too?"

"Yes, I wonder, but some people just take the legends for granted—especially the one about the orgies. In fact, there are some on the fringes of the 'international set' who come to Capri occasionally to continue what they think is the tradition."

A flash of surprise appeared on Leigh's face.

"You mean they have—have orgies here? Now?" she exclaimed softly. "How do you know?"

"If you're asking me if I've ever attended one then the answer is no," Marc said, grinning down at her. "I prefer more privacy. But how about you?"

"How about me, what?"

"Do you prefer privacy or does the idea of orgies appeal to you?"

"Of course not!" she gasped, her cheeks flaming. "You can't really think I—"

"No, I can't really think that at all, and I don't," he murmured, slipping his hand beneath her hair on her nape. Tilting her head back, he forced her to look at him. "You really should learn to recognize when I'm only teasing you."

"Maybe you should just stop teasing me!" she retorted. "Have you ever thought of that?"

"Not really." Laughing softly at her, he placed a kiss on the tip of her small nose. "How can I resist when you blush so charmingly?"

His smile was irresistible and she found herself smiling back despite a firm resolution to glare at him indignantly, and when his hand left the warm nape of her neck to close around her fingers in a gentle grip, she walked with him beyond the villa, through a grove of carob trees. He led her up to the edge of a cliff which dropped off sheerly, nearly a thousand feet to the sea below.

"There's also the legend that Tiberius forced his ex-favorites to jump off this cliff," Marc informed her, then shrugged. "Of course, some historians discount that too."

Wrapping her fingers tightly around his hand, Leigh leaned out over the cliff to stare at the swirling waters below, but the sight was so dizzying that she pulled back immediately.

"I think someone would have to give me a shove to

get me started before I'd ever jump," she said weakly. "Even if an emperor had ordered me to do it."

"No, you'd never obey orders blindly, would you, Leigh?" he asked softly, leading her away from the edge and back through the trees. "You have a mind of your own, don't you?"

"Well, I certainly hope so. I'd hate to be one of those people who does things just because almost everyone else is doing them."

"Then why are you—" Marc's words halted abruptly and he released her hand. "Oh, never mind. Well, is there something you'd like to do now, or would you like to take a walk along the beach at Marina Grande while we wait for the launch to return from Ischia?"

"That sounds fine to me," she murmured, bewildered by the sudden coolness she detected in his voice. And the silence that followed as they drove back down the mountain to the harbor did nothing to ease her mind.

He said nothing even as they walked along Marina Grande's coarse sand and pebbled beach that sloped steeply to the creaming surf. Finally, disconcerted by the inexplicable, silent treatment, Leigh wandered away from him, slipping out of her leather sandals to wade in the soft warm waves that lapped gently on the gray-brown beach. Wondering if she had done something to irritate him, she followed him with her eyes as he approached an outcropping of rocks up the pebbly incline. He stopped to lean back against one of the boulders, his feet slightly apart, his hands thrust deeply into the pockets of his trousers and, almost as if he sensed her watching him, he looked up. His narrowed gaze swept slowly over her, lingering for a long moment on her bare feet and suddenly he smiled, one of those lazy, evocative smiles.

Every nerve in her seemed to leap in response to that smile and she was powerless to prevent herself from going to him, but she kept her head bent and her legs were ridiculously weak and shaky.

"You don't care much for shoes, do you?" he asked softly, touching one finger beneath her chin to tilt her face up. "I've noticed that you slide your feet out of them every chance you get. Does that mean you're a free spirit?"

Suddenly very nervous, she couldn't find the words to give him an answer. Avoiding his eyes, she looked up and down the nearly deserted beach, moistening dry lips with the tip of her tongue, when she realized how effectively the outcropping of rocks seemed to isolate them.

"I wonder how Angelica and Sophia are doing," she murmured, simply to break the disturbing silence. "I hope they'll be okay."

Marc's finger beneath her chin began to trace light, teasing circles down the soft sensitive skin of her throat.

"Didn't I tell you the two of them would be just fine?" he whispered. "Stop worrying about them."

"But I'm just afraid Signora Cavalli is very angry at us for missing the launch—that she may be very impatient with Angelica because of it."

"After the little talk I had with Sophia before lunch, I think she knows she'd better be very nice to Angelica today," Marc said confidently. "When I really try, I can usually make her listen to reason."

"Why? Why will she listen to you?" Leigh asked impulsively and immediately wished she hadn't, because she had found it impossible to control the suspicious note in her voice. Now Marc's jaw had tightened and his green eyes were glittering dangerously.

"Is that another one of your veiled insinuations that I'm Angelica's real father?" he questioned her harshly, clamping rough hard fingers on her shoulders, pressing them down into the delicate bones. "Because if it is,

I'm telling you right now that I've had more than enough of your silly suspicions."

"But—but are they that silly?" Leigh persisted foolishly. "Something makes Signora Cavalli very obedient to you."

"But it isn't because I'm the father of her child," he said curtly, jerking her closer. "She just knows not to push me too far—but you obviously don't know that, even after what happened the other night in your room. You had a narrow escape then, but this time may be different."

"Oh what nonsense," Leigh said shakily, twisting in a futile effort to free herself. "You don't scare me any more with your outrageous remarks. Maybe I *am* beginning to know when you're only joking."

"Then maybe it's time you also learned to know when I'm not, because I wasn't joking then, *bambina mia,*" he told her, his voice a deep, throaty growl in her ear. "And I think you know very well that I wasn't, don't you? You know how very easy it would be for me to make love to you?"

"It would not either!" she protested defensively. "You'd need my cooperation, and you most certainly wouldn't get it!"

"You think not?" he asked mockingly, hard fingers holding the back of her head as his mouth lowered to nearly touch hers. "I believe you would cooperate, Leigh, so why don't we just see who's right."

His warm breath drifting across her lips sent a violent tremor over her body, and, unable to breathe, she awaited the touch of his mouth. He kept her waiting, smiling knowingly, his eyes half-closed and glimmering green as his fingers slid beneath the narrow straps of her denim sundress. He probed the tiny hollows between her delicate bones, exploring her slowly, watching her blue eyes widen as he pushed the straps aside and they dropped off her shoulders down around her upper arms. His gaze lowered to the deep, scented hollow between her breasts, exposed as the bodice of her dress slipped lower, and as he encircled her waist with one arm, his other hand trailed from her throat to the enticing swell of satiny flesh above her bra.

Trembling, she finally breathed again.

"Marc, no!" she whispered fiercely, but the moment her lips parted his descended, brushing against the softness. His teeth closed on her lower lip gently tugging, and as he whispered her name, the tip of his tongue moved from corner to sensitized corner of her mouth.

Leigh moaned softly, clutching at the soft fabric of his white challis shirt. His firm chest was unyielding beneath the heels of her small hands. And as his kiss deepened, became a hungry taking of her lips, her legs buckled beneath her. The arm round her waist caught her close against him, lifting her until only the tips of her toes still touched the coarse sand.

"Hold me," he commanded hoarsely. When her arms suddenly clasped tightly round his neck and her soft curves pressed, then yielded to him, his hand closed on the rounded, firm flesh of her hips. Iron hardness surged against her and as he widened his stance, bringing her closer still, his throbbing strength inflamed her senses almost like an act of possession itself. Playing with her lips, he lowered the back zipper of her dress as he drew her farther into the tiny, secluded cove the rocks encircled.

Before she could resist or even want to, the denim sundress was falling down round her feet. As he swept her up in his arms only to lay her down on the warm sand, she dug her nails into the taut muscles of his shoulders.

"Don't stop," she whispered, feeling a fleeting, intense anguish as his mouth left hers for a moment. "Kiss me again. Please."

"My sweet Leigh," he murmured then ravished her parted lips as his hand slipped under her back. Unsteady fingers unfastened the clip of her brief bra, and with a muffled exclamation, he tossed the scrap of diaphanous lace aside.

The gentle breeze couldn't cool her burning skin and she knew only his touch would ease the swelling ache in her breasts, but he didn't touch her. Drawing away slightly, he surveyed her with darkening eyes. Her breath caught in her throat. Never had she felt so delightfully vulnerable and she closed her eyes as desire awakened, sharp and unrelenting, inside her.

"You are exquisite," he whispered, his hands caressing her slim waist. "How could you give such a beautiful body to a boasting little boy like your Stefano?"

Leigh shook her head, but as she started to voice a denial Marc's fingertips grazed her breasts. She gasped softly as sensual delight danced over her skin, sweeping all thoughts of Stefano away. Marc's hands closed over her firm fullness, and as her nipples hardened against his palms, his fingers pressed roughly into her. Her eyes flickered open again to watch as he lowered his head to close white strong teeth on one dark, swollen peak—then the other. His tongue tasted her satiny skin before his seeking mouth closed hungrily, taking possession of one throbbing breast. She arched against him, lost in incredibly intense sensations, and her hands inside his shirt next to his heated flesh kneaded the corded muscles of his broad back. As the weight of his body pressed her down into the sand, her legs tangled with his.

"You're so warm," he groaned as his mouth left her breast to cover her parted lips for a savage moment. Propped on one elbow, he brushed a wispy tendril of hair back from her cheek as his other hand drifted downward. His fingers tugged at the soft nylon of her panties and hard knuckles grazed the bare, exquisitely sensitive skin of her abdomen.

Leigh stiffened instinctively with a gasp as her

fevered emotions were overwhelmed by the realization of what was about to happen. Suddenly scared and half-ashamed, she pushed at his chest. "No! No, I can't let you," she whispered frantically. "Marc, please, I can't."

"You can't stop me. You don't really want to," he said huskily against her throat. "You can't stop me, Leigh, not after letting it go this far."

"But I didn't mean for it to! It just happened so—so fast and now—now—oh, I'm sorry but I can't."

"But I can't let you go! God! Don't you know what you're doing to me?" With those tortured words, he pinned her hands above her head. "Don't fight me. Let me be gentle with you. I don't want to hurt you."

With her heart pounding in her ears, she hardly heard him, and she was completely unaware of the tears that began streaming down her cheeks until he lifted his head with a groan of defeat.

"My God, you play rough, don't you?" he muttered, shaking his head derisively. "What's a man supposed to do when a woman resorts to tears, Leigh? Rape her? Well rape has never appealed to me, so you can go back to your Stefano with a clear conscience. But for God's sake, from now on stay the hell away from me!"

As he pushed himself away and rose to his feet, shame washed over her. What she had done had been despicable and unforgivable. Since he had no idea that she was completely inexperienced and totally ignorant about men, he had every right to think she was nothing more than a tease. Gazing up miserably at the straight implacable line of his back, she wanted to try to explain—but no words would come.

"Get your clothes on before I change my mind," he commanded harshly as he strode away. "God, Leigh, don't you know you're driving me crazy?"

Watching him go, she found her bra and put it on with shaky fingers. She forced herself to get up, then stood for a moment clutching her sundress against her breasts. A sad little smile trembled on her lips, then vanished. If he thought she was driving him crazy, then what the devil did he imagine he was doing to her?

Chapter Seven

Early the next afternoon, Leigh sat on the piazza staring glumly at the orange grove. Angelica had gone to the kitchen to get Camellia a saucer of milk, and without the girl's chatter to provide a diversion, Leigh's thoughts were centered on Marc and on the events of the preceding day. After the episode on the beach he had spoken to her only when necessary, and the two hours they had waited for the launch to return from Ischia had seemed like an eternity. Then, when Angelica and Sophia arrived the tension only increased, since Sophia looked as if one wrong word to her would set her off on a tirade. Consequently, there was hardly any conversation among the three adults during the ride home to the villa, and only Angelica's excited chatter about her day of sightseeing had saved dinner from becoming a total disaster.

Now, as an oriole sang out from his branch on a carob tree, Leigh sighed dejectedly. Though she hadn't seen Marc all morning, or even at lunch, she wasn't at all certain that was a blessing. Since she had to face him sooner or later anyway, perhaps it would be less nerve-racking to simply get it over with. Perhaps he wasn't even irritated with her any more. After all, his emotions hadn't taken a bruising yesterday afternoon. He had wanted her to satisfy his most superficial physical desires, nothing more. So surely his masculine pride hadn't been wounded very deeply. Perhaps, if she was very lucky he would actually forget what had happened and would begin to be friendly to her again.

"Dreamer," she called herself bleakly. It was not realistic to expect him to be friendly when she had so much going against her. First she had tried to deceive him about her age, then had acted no better than a common little tease yesterday. No, considering her behavior, she had no right to expect him to be friendly. She supposed she would be fortunate if he managed to treat her civilly for the next few weeks.

Thoroughly depressed, Leigh rested her elbows on her knees, cupped her chin in her hands, and stared at a tiny ant making his way to the edge of the piazza. Lost in thought, she was slow to react when she heard the rapid staccato of spike heels against the tile, but finally she turned reluctantly, forcing a wan smile as Sophia approached.

"Where is my daughter?" the older woman asked haughtily, adjusting the lapels of her yellow designer suit. "I thought it was your duty to stay with her at all times."

"She's in the kitchen," Leigh explained, ignoring the insinuation that she was shirking her duty. "She wanted to get some milk for her kitten."

"That nasty creature!" Sophia whispered with a shudder, then glared at Leigh. "I suppose it was your idea for Angelica to take that dirty animal into her bedroom at night. Really, *signorina,* it was very irresponsible of you to even give her that cat."

Leigh's brows lifted in surprise. "I don't think it was

irresponsible, Signora Cavalli. That kitten has been good for Angelica. She seems much happier now than she ever did before."

Sophia smirked. "And why should you care whether she is happy or not? She is nothing to you."

"I happen to be very fond of Angelica," Leigh said stiffly, every muscle in her body tensing. "And I wouldn't be much of a companion if I didn't do everything I could to make her happy, would I?"

"Come now *signorina,* you do not fool me," Sophia retorted hatefully, placing her hands on her boyishly slim hips. "I know very well that you are far more interested in impressing Marc than you are in my daughter's happiness. You only pretend to be devoted to her because you think that will make him notice you. You are very transparent, Signorina Sheridan, and it was quite obvious to me yesterday that Angelica's happiness means nothing to you. You missed that launch deliberately, and you made Marc miss it too so you could be alone with him."

"I'm sorry you think that because it simply isn't true," Leigh replied as calmly as possible, striving to hold her temper in check. Lifting her chin she met the woman's eyes directly and reiterated, "I had nothing whatsoever to do with our missing that launch."

Sophia laughed unpleasantly. "It does you no good to lie to me. One woman can see through another so easily. You deliberately waited until the last minute to make your purchases in that trashy little shop and you pretended you needed Marc's help to deal with the proprietor so he would miss the boat with you and you would then have him all to yourself. What a pity you went to all that trouble for nothing, *signorina.* Obviously Marc saw through your silly little act too, because he certainly did not seem very pleased with you when Angelica and I arrived back from Ischia."

"But that wasn't because he—" Leigh halted abruptly, unwilling to divulge Marc's real reason for being angry at her.

"You see, you cannot even deny it," Sophia said smugly, misinterpreting Leigh's hesitation. "You were silly, *signorina,* to believe you could fool Marc with such an obvious ploy. He is a sophisticated man who has no patience with juveniles and their tricks."

Then why on earth does he tolerate an adolescent like you? Leigh longed to retort, but before she could say anything at all Angelica was wheeling herself out onto the piazza, and the deathly pallor of her face captured Leigh's complete attention. Ignoring Sophia, she rushed to meet the chair, bending over the child to press her hand against her forehead.

"You're so pale, Angelica," she exclaimed worriedly. "What's wrong? Don't you feel well?"

As if she hadn't heard the question, the girl stared past her at her mother. "Why is all your luggage in the *salon,* Mama?" she asked, her voice quavering. "You are not going to leave so soon, are you?"

"I am going, yes," Sophia answered breezily, patting the shining cap of her black hair with her fingertips. "Months ago I promised my friend Deidre that I would attend her masquerade ball."

"But—but, yesterday you told me you would stay here and visit with me for another week," Angelica reminded her, a pitiful note of supplication in her voice. "Remember? That is what you told me."

"I know I did, *bambina mia,* but the ball had completely slipped my mind." Sophia shrugged carelessly. "I only remember that it was to be this Saturday after I consulted my calendar last night."

"It is only Wednesday though, Mama, so you do not have to go yet, do you? Please stay. We had such a good time together yesterday and I—"

With an impatient toss of her hand Sophia answered in rapid Italian, and the frown between her brows deepened when her daughter was unable to lower her eyes quickly enough to conceal the tears that immediately sprang to them.

"You are not going to cry, are you?" the mother asked with a sigh. "You know that it upsets me terribly when you do. Besides, why are you so sad? I will come back to see you soon."

"How soon?" Angelica muttered, her chin nearly resting on her chest. "Will you promise to come back the day after the ball?"

Wearing one of those less than sincere smiles, Sophia came to brush a kiss across her daughter's thin cheek. "Well, I did not mean I would be back quite that soon, *bambina mia,*" she said lightly. "Deidre has asked me to be her houseguest all next week."

"Then you could stay here until Friday at least, if the ball is not until Saturday night," Angelica suggested hopefully. "You do not have to leave today."

"But I must go to Rome and be fitted for a costume. And there are a million other things that I must do."

Angelica seemed to shrink visibly in her chair, though she was not completely defeated yet. Her large black eyes sought her mother's face rather desperately as she whispered, "Then perhaps I could go to Rome with you. Just—just until Saturday. We could go shopping together. It would be fun and I would be no trouble for you."

As Leigh watched this exchange she was certain she saw something almost like panic flicker momentarily in Sophia's eyes, and even when the woman masked that initial reaction and shook her head, the impression of fear still lingered. Suddenly, surprisingly, Leigh felt sorry for the woman. She was afraid of her own child.

"Mama, please," Angelica whispered, giving it one more try. "Just stay one more day then. Just one more."

"Signora Cavalli," the housekeeper called from the

open doors to the sitting room. "Your taxi has come."

"I will be right there. Tell him to take my luggage," Sophia answered swiftly, unable to disguise the relief in her voice. Then, almost as if she were uncertain of the procedure, she gripped her daughter's shoulders and pulled her clumsily to her for a brief hug and her kiss lingered longer than usual against the girl's cheek. "I will be back in a couple of weeks, I promise, *piccola*. So you be a very nice girl and don't give Marc any trouble. All right?" Without waiting for an answer she then rushed away.

For a long moment after she was gone, Angelica only stared silently into space, but at last a desolate little smile hovered on her lips and she said softly, "I guess she was just pretending she was happy to be with me yesterday. I should have known that she could not suddenly begin to love me but—"

"I think she does love you but doesn't know quite how to show it," Leigh suggested, squeezing the girl's thin shoulder. "Parents have problems too, Angelica. They aren't perfect, and sometimes they have to straighten out their own lives before they have a lot of time for their children."

Angelica shook her head doubtingly. "Was there ever a time when your parents did not have time for you and your brothers?"

"Occasionally," Leigh answered truthfully. "Sometimes they had problems we couldn't understand and they were short-tempered with us. But that didn't mean they didn't love us any more."

"But Mama has never had time for me," Angelica said dully, staring at her hands lying limply in her lap. She shrugged as that hopeless little smile once again appeared on her lips. "When I was a little girl, I would lie in bed at night at the convent and wonder what it would be like to be a part of a family with a mother and a father and brothers and sisters. Some of the girls who went to school there went home every afternoon, and I visited a few times with some of them but—but it was not like having a real home of my own."

Knowing words couldn't help at the moment, Leigh kept silent, her hand still resting comfortingly on Angelica's shoulder. It took a great deal of self-restraint not to cry for the girl who seemed to have gone beyond the point where she could cry for herself. Several long minutes passed and finally Leigh realized this was not one of those depressions Angelica could snap out of by herself. She needed help. On impulse, Leigh went to the small table in front of them and picked up the brightly colored hair ribbons Angelica had bought on Ischia the day before. Choosing a long narrow pink grosgrain, she hurried back behind the girl's chair.

"Let's see what your hair will look like with this ribbon threaded through one long braid. As thick and long as it is, I bet it will really look pretty. Don't you?"

"Perhaps, but—but maybe I would look nicer if I had my hair cut very short like Mama's," Angelica murmured, glancing up at Leigh hopefully. "What do you think?"

"I think it's beautiful just the way it is. Maybe someday when you're older you'll want to have it cut short, but for now I would leave it the way it is, if I were you. I certainly wish mine was as long, thick and lovely as yours."

"But you have very beautiful hair, Leigh. It looks like sunshine," Angelica said sweetly and sincerely. "You do not really wish your hair was like mine. Men like girls with hair the color of yours." Suddenly a barely discernible trace of a mischievous twinkle shone in her green eyes. "Perhaps that is what we should do to my hair, hmmm. Leave it long but make it blond instead of dark."

"Good Lord, no!" Leigh responded. "I have no desire to be murdered, which is what would happen to me if Marc saw that I'd let you bleach your hair. So let's just leave the color the way it is and change it by braiding this ribbon through it instead. Okay?"

Ten minutes later, Leigh stepped back to survey her handiwork.

"It looks terrific, Angie," she announced truthfully. "If you wanted to, you could go to a party with it arranged that way."

"May I see it, please?" the girl asked. "You could bring me that small mirror that hangs on the wall in the salon."

Happy to do anything that would keep Angelica's mind off her mother, Leigh hurried into the house, borrowed the gold-framed mirror, then rushed back through the sitting room, nearly stumbling over Camellia snoozing in a patch of sunlight in front of one of the wide, tall windows.

"You can't sleep your entire life away," she said, picking up the cat. "Your mistress could use a bit of cheering—so open your eyes and try to be entertaining." Though Camellia only blinked up at her unenthusiastically, she took her out onto the piazza anyway.

A moment later, Angelica had the braid pulled over one shoulder and was carefully surveying her reflection in the mirror. "Why, it does look a little pretty," she said, obviously surprised. Then she sighed and her shoulders drooped again. "But I will probably never wear my hair this way very often. I do not go to parties."

"Why don't you ask your uncle to take you out to dinner then?" Leigh suggested. "I'm sure he'd be honored to escort a lovely young lady like you anywhere."

"But Mama told me not to bother him."

"But I'm sure he wouldn't mind taking you to dinner. He—" Leigh's words trailed off as the younger girl shook her head glumly and began stroking Camellia with a faraway look in her eyes. Unwilling to let her slip back into a deep depression, Leigh picked out a length of wide pink satin ribbon from the basket on the table and without a word, tied it loosely around the kitten's neck. Unperturbed, Camellia sat on Angelica's lap, licking her paws. It was obvious that she was completely indifferent to the large bow that adorned her. Angelica, however, was smiling again.

"Oh, she is beautiful—the most beautiful kitten in the world," she whispered softly, nuzzling her cheek against Camellia's soft thick fur. "I wonder if she would let us put a ribbon on her every day so she will always look this pretty."

"I wouldn't count on that," Leigh said wryly. "Cats can be so fickle sometimes that she might not even let us put a ribbon on her tomorrow—or ever again, for that matter. But," she added when Angelica sighed disappointedly, "I'm sure Marc would take some pictures of her right now so you could always remember what she looks like with her bow—even if she won't allow us to put one on her again. Why don't you ask him if he will."

"But Mama said not to bother him."

"He wouldn't mind taking a few pictures. I know he wouldn't."

"Then would you ask him for me? *Please.*"

Leigh hesitated, not exactly eager to seek Marc out after what had happened between them yesterday afternoon. But the uncertainty in Angelica's eyes overrode all personal considerations. If he could do anything to boost his niece's spirits she had to ask him to do it. "All right," she agreed at last. "I'll ask him."

"Now?"

"Yes, now," Leigh muttered reluctantly. With her stomach already beginning to knot, she walked away.

The red light above the darkroom door was shining when she walked into Marc's study. For a moment she hovered by his desk, unable to decide whether to wait or leave and come back again later.

"I'll wait five minutes," she compromised aloud. Too

nervous to sit, she went to peruse the contents of one of the ceiling-high bookcases, and was rather surprised to learn that Marc had so many diverse interests. She had incorrectly assumed that most of his books dealt with photography. Instead, he had collections on oceanography, ancient history, and sociology, plus large selections of fiction and even poetry.

Shaking her head, she wondered if she would ever be able to understand him. Every day she knew him he seemed to become increasingly more complex. His relationship with Sophia baffled her, and to add to her confusion she recalled what Stefano had told her about the married starlet he had been romancing a few months ago. Somehow he simply didn't seem the type who would relish an affair with another man's wife. He seemed more intrinsically honest than that. Certainly, he never minded telling her the truth about what he thought of her, so she couldn't imagine him being less than honest with anyone else. Of course, she could very well be wrong. She hardly knew him, and he did have a very winning personality. She had always heard the real charmers were the ones that couldn't quite be trusted. Nevertheless, she was certain his affection for Angelica was genuine. Yet, after several more minutes of trying to analyze him, she finally sighed in disgust. Perhaps it would be easier to simply resign herself to never understanding him. Perhaps he was just too sophisticated for her unworldly comprehension.

She glanced at her wristwatch and when she saw that she had already waited more than five minutes she decided to leave and return later. When she started to go out, however, the door to the darkroom opened and Marc came out.

"Did you want to see me about something?" he asked brusquely, icy green eyes piercing hers. And when she hesitated and gestured uncertainly, he added, "I'm very busy so if you have something to say, just say it."

Despite his obvious hostility, Leigh explained to him about the kitten. After stressing how much Angelica wanted him to take some photographs she concluded by saying, "I know you said you're very busy, but if you could just take the time to make a few pictures I think it would help Angelica so much. I'm really worried about her. I've never seen her as depressed as she is now."

"Depressed? Why?" Marc questioned, with a perplexed frown. "Yesterday she seemed very happy—so what's happened to upset her today?"

"Her mother's leaving, of course. What else did you think it could—"

"Her mother's leaving?" Marc repeated violently, taking a step forward. "Are you telling me that Sophia has left this house? She packed her things and actually left?"

"Well, yes. I thought you knew. I mean—" Leigh's words trailed off and her cheeks flushed crimson at the string of uncomplimentary expletives he uttered. And when he began to move toward her she retreated several steps backward, fearing he meant to direct his fury at her.

"When did she leave?" he asked, his jaw clenched. "And where the hell was she going?"

"She left over an hour ago and planned to stop in Rome before going on to visit with some friend named Deidre," Leigh told him hastily. "She said she might be back in a couple of weeks."

"Damn her. I told her in no uncertain terms that she was to stay here with Angelica for at least two weeks." Thrusting his hands into his pockets, he shook his head in Leigh's general direction. "Devoted little mother, isn't she?"

"I think she's scared of being close to Angelica," Leigh said softly. "She almost acts as if she has no idea how to love her."

"I never realized how perceptive you are," he commented, a faint smile restoring some warmth to his eyes. Then he lifted a detaining hand. "Wait here. I'll get a camera."

A moment later Leigh smiled tentatively up at him as he took her elbow to guide her out of the study and down the hall. "I know what you said about being busy but I wonder if—if maybe you could take time out some evening this week and take Angelica to dinner," she suggested hopefully. "If you could, I think it would help her so much. When Signora Cavalli left today, she just seemed to feel no one in the world cared what happened to her."

"What about you? Doesn't she know you care?"

"I'm not family, though. I'm only a paid companion and that's not the same."

Marc nodded. "Yes, I suppose you're right. Well, I see no reason why I can't take the two of you out to dinner. In fact, any evening this week is fine with me."

"Oh, but I didn't ask you to take her out because I wanted to be invited to go along too," Leigh said hastily. "Oh no, I just thought you would want to do anything you could to get her out of this deep depression."

"I know that, Leigh. It never occurred to me that you might be fishing for an invitation," Marc responded indulgently. "I asked you to join us because I'm sure Angelica would like for you to."

"Oh. Oh, I see," Leigh murmured, relieved that he hadn't felt compelled to invite her, yet slightly disappointed too because he had only asked her to please his niece. Yet she knew she had no reason to hope he would ever desire her company again after the disaster of yesterday afternoon. In fact, she was lucky he even wanted her to remain here as Angelica's companion. Telling herself she had better be grateful that he was at least civil to her today, she preceded him out onto the piazza where the photography session immediately began.

After shooting countless pictures of Angelica and her

kitten, Marc stopped to stare thoughtfully at his niece for a moment. "How would you like to be the photographer for a while?" he asked finally, holding out the expensive, yet uncomplicated camera to the girl. "I think you'd really enjoy shooting pictures, *piccola.* In fact, it could turn into a very exciting hobby."

"Me? Really?" Angelica whispered incredulously, taking the camera as if she feared it might break. Gazing lovingly up at her uncle she smiled shyly. "You really think I could make some nice pictures? Do you think I could possibly ever be as good a photographer as you are?"

"It started out as a hobby for me too, you know, and if I remember correctly I was about the same age." Marc leaned over the wheelchair, pointing out features of the camera. "Now this is the lens adjustor, but we won't worry about that yet."

As he went on with a patient explanation, Leigh stood at a distance and watched. When he was being as kind as he was right now she found him nearly irresistible, and in that moment she thought she would have given almost anything to go back to yesterday afternoon and change the way it had ended. What would it have been like to have given herself completely to him? Would she have regretted it bitterly later, when he was no longer interested in her? Or would she have always treasured the memory of his lovemaking? Once, only a few weeks ago, the answer to that question would have been obvious. She would have been certain she would regret a brief summer love affair. But a few weeks ago she had not yet met Marc, and meeting him seemed to be slowly altering her entire philosophy. It was disturbing, to say the least. No other man had ever tempted her to re-evaluate her self-imposed sexual restrictions as Marc was tempting her to now. Though that worried her enough, she was far more concerned about becoming too emotionally involved with him. The attraction she felt was no longer merely physical. She had begun to like and respect him, even if she wasn't completely sure she could trust him.

Staring at the muscular lines of his broad back as he leaned over his niece, Leigh shook herself mentally, trying to dispel the memory of the feel of his heated flesh beneath her fingers. It wasn't so easy to forget, however. For the first time in her life she had enjoyed touching a man, and as she recalled the heavy strength of his body as he had pressed her down into the sand, she was lost for a moment in the reminiscence. It was finally the sound of Angelica's voice saying her name that brought her back to reality.

"Uncle Marcus says you should pose for me," the girl was saying. "So stand very still and look pretty."

With Marc observing, Leigh couldn't relax and her cheeks felt tight as she forced a smile.

"That is not a very good smile," Angelica complained from behind the camera. "Uncle Marcus will you stand beside her and say something funny so she will smile better? Put your arm around her waist."

"Oh, that's not necessary," Leigh murmured as he joined her and immediately obeyed his niece's instructions. "You don't have to—"

"Always obey the photographer," he whispered, drawing her close against him. "Now relax and smile like you mean it."

"Kiss her this time Uncle Marcus," Angelica instructed a moment later. "Then it will not matter if she does not smile."

"Angelica, that's silly," Leigh began weakly. "Your uncle doesn't want—"

"He has kissed you before. I saw from my balcony when you were in the garden the other day."

"Children see everything. Didn't you know that?" he asked softly, smiling indulgently as Leigh blushed. "So why fight it?" Cupping her slender neck in both his hands, his thumbs tilting her chin up, he lowered his mouth to hers.

Having expected a light brief kiss of no consequence, Leigh was not prepared for the subtle demands his mouth made. Though he didn't draw her closer, his lips were hard and seeking as they slowly enticed hers to part. When he released her finally, meeting her bemused gaze with an evocative smile, her heart was beating with the oddest irregularity.

"Ooh, that was a good shot," Angelica announced excitedly. "Kiss her again, Uncle Marcus."

"My pleasure," he whispered so only Leigh could hear. But before she could utter a protest, or he could lower his head again, the moment was interrupted.

"*Scusi,* Signor Cavalli," the housekeeper spoke from the doorway to the salon. "But there is a visitor for Signorina Sheridan."

"A visitor?" Leigh exclaimed bewilderedly. "For me?"

"*Si.* A young gentleman, *signorina.*"

Stefano! Leigh knew instanteously that was who it must be and, judging by the sudden tensing of Marc's body, he obviously knew it too. After asking for his understanding with a beseeching little smile, she turned away and walked reluctantly across the piazza.

"*Carissima!*" Stefano greeted her effusively, striding across the room to envelop her in an unwelcome embrace. "*Bella mia,* I have missed you," he whispered, nuzzling her ear, then suddenly tensing. "Where are your glasses and why are you dressed that way?"

"That silly disguise didn't fool anybody for long," she replied lightly, wishing he would release her. "So I decided to be myself again."

"And Cavalli didn't fire you when he realized how young you are?" Stefano queried suspiciously. "Why?"

"Angelica was beginning to depend on me, I guess. He didn't want to upset her."

"You're certain that was his only reason?" Pulling away slightly, Stefano stared broodingly at her. "And what was your reason for not calling and arranging to meet me on Sunday?"

Freeing herself from his arms hastily, she explained, "I wanted to stay with Angelica. She was feeling very lonely."

"But you should not be expected to work all the time," he protested testily. "Sunday is your day off. That was the arrangement."

"No one asked me to work Sunday," she told him firmly. "I chose to stay with Angelica. Her mother was supposed to be here with her but she wasn't so—"

"You are too good, *bella mia,* at least to other people." Stefano sighed dramatically. "To me you are very, very cruel."

"Oh, don't exaggerate," she muttered, beginning to lose patience. "Just tell me why you've come here today."

"Good news, *cara!* Very good news!" he announced proudly. "I have found you a position on the staff of one of the news services. Or rather, my father found it. Is that not the best news you have ever been given?"

Leigh stared at him, not knowing exactly what to say. Three weeks ago his news would have been cause for a grand celebration, but now the situation wasn't so simple. She didn't see how she could possibly walk out on Angelica now, especially since Sophia had deserted her today.

"Say something, *cara mia,*" Stefano prompted after a long moment. "What is it? Are you so excited that you cannot speak?"

"It isn't that. Oh, Stefano, I—" Pausing, she took a deep breath, then blurted out, "I can't leave here yet. Angelica really needs me."

"But this job is just what you wanted and I had to exaggerate your qualifications to my father so he would get it for you. You must take it now!" Stefano glared at her. "Are you sure you want to stay for the sake of the child?" he asked sharply. "Or is the uncle who interests you?"

"You're being ridiculous," she muttered evasively, turning her back on him. "Angelica is a lonely, disturbed child. Since she's finally beginning to trust me, I think it could hurt her very badly if I left now. And, after all, I took this job knowing I was expected to stay at least two months. It wouldn't be very considerate of me to just walk out on them now."

"*Them, cara?*" Stefano questioned sarcastically. "So it is not only for the girl that you stay?"

"Oh, stop making silly insinuations!"

Stepping around in front her, Stefano grasped her shoulders, muttering, "Insinuations? This Marcus Cavalli is a very attractive man, is he not? And you are a beautiful girl. What is your relationship with him? Or would it be better for me not to know?"

"Enough," Leigh commanded stiffly, jerking free of his grasp. "You don't own me, Stefano, and I don't have to put up with your insulting insinuations. I think you'd better just leave now."

"You are going with me, *cara.*"

"No I am not! I just told you I can't desert Angelica. I'd never be able to live with my conscience if I walked out on her."

"Go pack," Stefano persisted pompously. "I am taking you away from the unhealthy influence of this Marcus Cavalli. I will await you in the car."

"You can sit in your car and wait until doomsday if you want to waste your time that way," she retorted. "But I will not be leaving here with you today and that's my final word."

"*Cara,* you are so obstinate," he murmured, moving swiftly to gather her to him in a tight embrace. "Trust me. You will be glad you left. This job I spoke of is just what you were seeking."

"Maybe so. It's a shame it wasn't available three

weeks ago," she said as patiently as possible, wriggling in an effort to free herself. "But it wasn't and I can't—"

"Miss Sheridan, Angelica is out on the piazza, not in here," Marc interrupted gruffly, striding into the room through the open French doors. His green eyes glittered icily as Leigh nervously disentangled herself from Stefano's arms. Then his gaze turned to the unwelcome visitor, "My niece relies on Leigh. I'm sure you understand," he declared mockingly, as if he didn't give a damn whether he was understood or not. "So, if you would be so kind—"

"Go, Stefano," Leigh whispered urgently. "We can talk some other time."

"I want you to come with me. Now."

"Please, just go."

Stefano's face darkened sullenly and he muttered before he walked away, "You will be hearing from me, Leigh. You can depend on that."

She watched him go, then with rising apprehension, turned back to face Marc. Her heart seemed to leap up into her throat when she found him standing directly behind her, close enough to touch.

"I—I didn't invite him here, honestly," she babbled, staring at the brown column of his neck to avoid meeting his eyes. "He just dropped by to—to say hello."

"And to try to get you to leave with him," Marc said harshly, gripping her waist roughly with both his hands. "Well, if you have any ideas about going soon, you'd better just put them out of your mind. I'm not about to let you leave Angelica right now, no matter how much you long to be with your lover."

"You have to be the most opinionated, infuriating man I've ever met in my life," she snapped right back, her temper exploding. "You don't have to forbid me to leave your niece. I'd never do that to her right now anyway! I happen to be very fond of her and I don't need you to be my conscience, thank you. You have a lot of nerve, do you know that? How dare you presume that I'd leave just because Stefano wants me to? He doesn't own me and I just told him that. I told him I couldn't possibly leave Angelica right now and he was wasting his time trying to persuade me to."

"I just bet you did," Marc retorted sarcastically. "If I hadn't interrupted, you would have been deciding on the best time to sneak away."

"*Ooh,* you're impossible," she whispered furiously, wrenching free to stand before him, rigid with indignation. "If you don't want to believe what I say, then don't. But I'll have you know I did tell Stefano that I would *not* go with him under any circumstances. Why else do you think he went sulking out of here like a silly little boy? Men! I'm beginning to think you're all alike."

Marc said nothing for a minute. Narrowed eyes flicked over her with scorching intensity, and when he spoke his voice was deceptively low and controlled. "Not quite alike, Leigh. Cross me and you'll find I can be more dangerous than your sulking Stefano—what *is* his name? He looks vaguely familiar."

"Marvini," she provided. "Stefano Marvini."

"Marvini! Umberto Marvini's son?" Marc questioned violently, his fingers digging into her waist. "And you still say you're not here to spy on me when your lover's father owns half the newspapers in Italy?" Green eyes blazed down at her. "Nothing, and I mean *nothing,* about my personal life better turn up as an item in one of those scandal sheets," he warned ominously. "If you dare hurt Angelica by sharing your ridiculous fantasy about my being her father, by God, I'll—"

"You'll what? Take me up to the cliff and force me to jump off the way the all-powerful Tiberius used to do any poor soul who happened to displease him?"

"Oh no, Leigh," Marc whispered, a cruel smile

making him look almost pagan. "Tossing you off a cliff would be a sinful waste. I assure you I could think of much more pleasurable ways to deal with you."

"Promises, promises," she taunted, then bit back a gasp as strong hands jerked her to him. Aqua eyes, flashing defiance, met the dark green of his, stare for stare. "If I were here to spy on you, do you think I would be fool enough to tell you Stefano's real last name?" she added succinctly. Just before Marc abruptly released her, for one fleeting moment, she imagined she saw something akin to confusion flit across his dark, lean face. But then it was gone, and she was no longer certain she had seen it at all.

Chapter Eight

"Could—Could I ask you something?" Angelica began uneasily, sitting in her chair in her bedroom watching Leigh rearrange the contents of a dresser drawer. "It is very very personal, *signorina.*"

The *signorina* immediately captured Leigh's full attention. Angelica never called her that anymore, so what she had to ask must be extremely important. Forsaking the contents of the drawer, she walked across the room to sit on the carved chest at the end of Angelica's canopied bed, next to the wheelchair.

"Ask away," she prompted, clasping her hands around her knees. "I just hope I have the answer."

Staring at the floor, Angelica cleared her throat nervously. "It is personal. It—it is about my body." Thin hands fluttered around in the general area of her chest. "I-I think I am growing again. They grew some two years ago, but not very much. Now they have grown more and sometimes they ache a little."

"You need a bra then," Leigh said matter-of-factly. "So we'll have to go into town and buy some."

"Oh, that is what I hoped you would say," Angelica said, her words coming in a rush of relief. "I mean, I hoped a bra would help. I was not sure. I was a little afraid that I ached because something was wrong. I am so glad there is not."

"That aching is perfectly normal," Leigh said gently. "But I do think a bra will be a great help. So why don't we ask Signor Rossetti to drive us to town today?"

"Oh, that would be wonderful. But do you think we could find some in my size that are pretty?" Angelica asked hopefully, then grimaced. "Some of the girls at the convent wore such ugly elastic looking things that just mashed everything down flat. I think I would rather ache than wear one of those."

"Oh, I remember those things," Leigh said laughingly. "You're right. They are ugly. And since they only squash everything down, I never understood their purpose. But I'm sure we can find you something much better, maybe something with just a touch of lace." Hopping up, she went back across the room to the dresser. "Let me finish straightening this drawer then I'll go tell the *signor* we'll need a ride to town."

"*Signorina?*" Angelica called softly a few moments later, and color darkened her cheeks when Leigh turned, her brows lifting inquiringly. "Uh, that other thing that happens to girls. It has not happened to me yet. The Sisters told us about it but—but I am not sure I will know what to do when it happens."

"Just tell me or Signora Rossetti," Leigh said over her shoulder, realizing fully for the first time how much a thirteen-year-old girl needed an older woman to talk to. "And don't panic."

"I will try not to. It makes me feel better to know that I will be able to tell Signora Rossetti or you," Angelica said softly. "I am so glad you are here, Leigh.

You make it easy for me to ask about things that bother me."

Closing the drawer, her task finished, Leigh smiled. "Well, I certainly don't mind your asking questions. And I'll always try to answer them if I can."

"Even if they are very personal?"

"Even then."

"Even if they are questions about you?"

At the teasing note in Angelica's voice, Leigh eyed her suspiciously. "I think I may be falling into a trap, but yes. You can ask me personal questions."

Angelica giggled mischievously behind her hand. "All right. I will test you. Did you like it when Uncle Marcus kissed you the other day?"

"Well, yes," Leigh admitted in an offhanded way. "I like being kissed."

"Especially by Uncle Marcus, hmmm? You like him?"

Leigh shrugged, trying to appear nonchalant. "Sure, I like him. He's a nice man."

"You like him more than you would most nice men though, do you not?" Angelica persisted perceptively. "Are you in love with him?"

"I—Well, I'm not sure I can answer that," Leigh murmured, realizing with great surprise that she really couldn't. "It's a difficult question."

"But you promised to try to answer any question I asked," the younger girl reminded her. "So? Are you in love with Uncle Marcus?"

"I guess I really don't know the answer," Leigh said, examining her fingernails abstractedly. "Maybe I'd better think it over, and after I've decided you'll be the first to know."

"Really, Leigh?" Angelcia grinned happily. "If you will tell me something so personal then that makes us friends, does it not?"

"Of course we're friends," Leigh answered, walking to the closet to get a dress for Angelica to wear into town. She hesitated a moment, then looked back over her shoulder. "Just remember, friends know how to keep secrets so I'll make a bargain with you. After I make my decision don't you tell your uncle what it is, and I won't tell him that underneath your blouses you're wearing a brand new sexy, lacy bra. A deal?"

"A deal," Angelica agreed, giggling for the first time in a way that made her sound almost happy.

Before dinner that evening, Leigh was sitting on the piazza when Angelica wheeled herself out, grinning excitedly.

"Oh, you've put on the blouse we bought you today," Leigh commented, nodding her approval of the white, sheer georgette fabric that accented the girl's dark skin and hair. "It looks terrific."

"Do you really think so?" Angelica's voice lowered to a whisper. "I am wearing one of the bras also. Does it make me look different?"

"You look very shapely, less like a little girl," Leigh assured her. "But how does the bra feel? Is it comfortable?"

"Well, it does feel a bit strange."

Leigh smiled wryly. "They take some getting used to, but at least your first one is nylon. My first was cotton and I was in such a rush to wear it I wouldn't let my mother wash the stiffness out of it. It felt like I'd wrapped stiff cardboard around myself. I could stand to wear it only a couple of hours that first time."

Angelica laughed, then sighed rather wistfully. "I like you to tell me things that happened to you when you were my age, but I do wish Mama would talk to me that way too. I wonder how she felt when she bought her first bra. I would like to know if she felt proud, and if she looked at herself in the mirror for a long time the way I did this afternoon. I would like to know if hers felt like stiff cardboard wrapped around her."

"You'll have to ask her when she comes back to see you."

"There is only one more week to wait until she comes," Angelica said eagerly. "Is that not right? You heard her promise to come back in two weeks?"

"Yes, I heard her." Now, let's just hope she keeps that promise, Leigh added silently.

"I just cannot wait to tell her about my bra," the girl chattered exuberantly. "She will be so surprised, I think. She believes I am still a baby, but this will show her that I am not." Her chattering ceased and she turned her head at the sound of footsteps inside the sitting room. "Uncle Marcus is coming. Oh, I wonder if he will notice the way I look."

Dressed casually in white, close-fitting slacks and a navy blue blazer, his light blue shirt open at the collar, Marc strode across the piazza toward them, stopping first at the portable bar Signora Rossetti had wheeled out earlier.

"Your usual glass of white wine, Leigh?" he asked, looking up briefly to acknowledge her affirmative answer with a nod. "How about you, Angelica? Some kind of fruit juice?"

"Yes, please, Uncle Marcus," his niece said, maneuvering her chair where he couldn't pass by without almost tripping over her. She sat tensed, her hands clutched around the armrests, waiting for him to really look at her and she almost seemed to radiate excitement. At last, when he smiled down at her and handed her a small tumbler of apricot juice, she grinned at him hopefully.

Obviously, he realized something was expected of him because his eyes narrowed for a fraction of a second, then lightened with recognition.

"That's a new blouse you have on, isn't it, *piccola?*" he asked observantly. "I like it very much. You look absolutely ravishing, my dear."

Laughing at his fairly good Cary Grant imitation,

Angelica lifted her arms out from her sides. "Do you notice anything else? Does my new blouse make me look different?"

Leaning idly on one elbow against the bar, he examined her carefully.

"Umm, there is something different about you," he said perceptively after a moment. "I'm not sure what it is—maybe you just look older somehow."

He had told her just what she wanted to hear. With a contented sigh, she took a sip of her juice, and over the rim of her glass her black eyes sparkled merrily at Leigh. Then, after putting her drink down on the bartop, she wheeled away toward the far end of the piazza where Camellia was stalking a grasshopper.

After handing Leigh her drink, Marc sat down close beside her on the steel-framed settee, his muscular thigh brushing against hers. For a moment he stared thoughtfully at his niece, then turned toward Leigh with a smile.

"Amazing, isn't it?" he remarked softly. "Our little girl is growing up."

"Our little girl?" Leigh questioned, her voice as soft as his had been as her wide aqua eyes explored his face. "You mean yours and mine?"

He nodded. "For the summer at least, she seems to be ours, doesn't she? Do you mind sharing a child with me?"

"N-no, I don't mind." Leigh swallowed with difficulty and averted her gaze, glad he couldn't know she was wondering how it would be to really share a child with him, their own child. Trying to push such fanciful thoughts aside, she fidgeted nervously, murmuring: "She does seem to have grown very quickly in the past few weeks, doesn't she? I mean emotionally, as well as physically."

"Of course I'd noticed the emotional growth. She acts much more mature now but—" Marc smiled rather sheepishly. "I have to admit it never occurred to me that she was going through physical changes as well. I imagine that's what precipitated that impromptu shopping trip today, right? Thank you for realizing she needed some—uh—additions to her wardrobe. I certainly never would have. She's lucky to have you."

His praise pleased her far more than she thought it should have, and she was relieved that the gathering dusk camoflaged the warm blush that crept into her cheeks. "I just wish I could be everything she needs, but I'm afraid I just can't be. She needs her mother."

Taking one of her small hands in both his, Marc whispered, "She seems to have adopted you as her mother, just the way she adopted me as her father. So be prepared—she may very well start telling strangers that she's really your daughter."

"Is that another way of saying she's no more your real daughter than she is mine?"

"Yes, I guess it is. I suppose you still don't believe me?"

"I don't know what to believe," Leigh whispered back, unable to tear her bewildered gaze away from the mysterious darkness of his. "I—I just don't know. She looks like you, and Sophia is a very beautiful woman who is obviously more interested in you as a man than as a brother-in-law."

"That doesn't necessarily mean the feeling is mutual."

"Doesn't it?"

"No, it doesn't and it isn't," he murmured, lowering his head to brush firm lips across one high cheekbone, then the other. "I make it a policy not to contend with more than one beautiful woman at a time, and at the moment, *bambina mia,* I'm having enough trouble with you."

"Me?" Leigh breathed, trembling as his mouth moved ever closer to her own. "But I'm just Angelica's companion. That's all I am here. How can I possibly be trouble for you?"

"Sometimes you seem like such an innocent," he said indulgently. "Don't you know how troubling it is for me to try to sleep every night, knowing you are just down the hall, all alone in that big bed?"

"But, I—"

"You know I want you, Leigh. You have to know that," he said against her lips, his warm breath filling her throat. "I think I began to want you even when you were still wearing those ridiculous dresses that I thought were concealing a pregnancy. I felt very protective toward you then, did you know that? But even so, I still wanted you. And now—"

As his mouth closed over hers, she moved instinctively into his arms, her heart pounding as she awaited the engulfing passion that always flared between them. Yet, somehow, there was more tenderness than passion in the kiss they were sharing, and she found herself responding to him uninhibitedly, without the slightest amount of fear that she might regret her eagerness later. This kiss seemed like a new beginning, one with the potential for providing a very satisfactory ending. But that illusion was shattered almost immediately.

"Marc, oh Marc darling, where are you?" a sugary feminine voice called through the deepening twilight. "The housekeeper said you were out here so where are you?"

"Holy heaven!" Marc groaned, dragging his lips from Leigh's. "She's finally found me."

At that moment, inside the house Signor Rossetti chose to flip the switch that illuminated the piazza with the light from several brass post lamps placed strategically among the bordering oleanders. Blinking, Leigh watched as Marc rose to his feet, then her eyes widened at the vision that was tripping lightly across the tile, toward them.

"Darling, you naughty thing," the woman in the scarlet silk suit chided as she flung herself into his arms. "Do you know I've been searching for you for the past three months? I know the situation with Arthur was getting pretty sticky, but really, you didn't have to hide yourself away from me too. Oh, I've missed you so. Have you missed me?"

Having heard the commotion, Angelica sped her chair directly to the scene, nearly screeching to a halt when she saw what was happening. Her mouth fell open in astonishment as she and Leigh exchanged incredulous glances.

For Leigh, incredulity changed very quickly to dismay. A heavy ache settled in her chest as she watched Marc disentangle himself from the arms of Brandi Wilkins, Hollywood's latest sex sensation. So much for a new beginning, she thought bleakly. The situation hadn't changed. Only the players had. Out with Sophia—the old competition—and in with Brandi Wilkins—the new. And seeing what a true, natural beauty Brandi was, Leigh knew it wouldn't be much of a competition at all.

"Brandi," Marc muttered rather uncomfortably, raking his fingers through his hair. "How have you been?"

"Out of my mind, wondering where you were, darling," she whispered petulantly, clinging to his arm. "But that doesn't matter now that I've found you. I have something much more important to tell you. I realized, finally, what you wanted me to do and I did it. I left Arthur and here I am!"

"Yes, so I see. But how did you find me?"

"Oh, a friend of mine in Rome saw an item in the newspaper—something about your cozy hideaway on Capri."

"Newspaper item," Marc repeated grimly, half turning toward Leigh.

As he glared at her accusingly she wanted to shake her head in denial, but the menacing look in his eyes was paralyzing. Yet she automatically gave him her hand when he held out his, knowing instinctively that he would make her regret it if she didn't. His fingers closed without gentleness around hers. He pulled her to her feet and she stood on rubbery legs beside him, afraid to guess what he was planning to do.

"Brandi, meet Leigh Sheridan and my niece, Angelica," he said at last. "Angelica, Leigh, I'm sure you recognize Brandi." Then, squeezing Leigh's fingers in his until her grandmother's pearl ring was cutting painfully into her flesh, he added calmly: "Congratulate me, Brandi. I'll be a married man soon. In fact, Leigh and I were just discussing where we want to spend our wedding trip."

Though Leigh's gasp caught in her throat and nearly choked her, Brandi's reaction was not suppressed. After the initial shock, she shook her head and pursed her lips in a disapproving moue.

"Don't tease me like that, darling," she whispered seductively. "I know you're impatient with me for waiting so long to leave Arthur, and I'm sorry I did wait, but you don't have to pretend you're going to marry someone else just to get back at me."

"I assure you I'm not pretending," he lied, smiling down at Leigh as he drew her closer to his side. "Leigh is my fiancée, aren't you, *bambina mia?*"

As Leigh realized he really meant to use her to make Brandi jealous, a sharp, unrelenting pain rippled through her chest down to knot her stomach, making her feel slightly nauseous. Yet the remnant of her pride refused to let him know he had hurt her. Rebellious, aqua eyes met his, but before she could dispute his claim, his fingers crushed hers in unmistakable warning. A muscle jerked in his clenched jaw, reminding her silently that he blamed her for the item in the Rome newspaper, and telling her that she would be unwise to make more trouble for herself. Suddenly, her resentment was overshadowed by a very basic fear of his superior physical strength and the potential for ruthlessness she had always suspected he possessed. So, though she despised herself for letting him use her, she turned to meet the startled confusion in Brandi's hazel eyes. Smiling as nonchalantly as she could she nodded.

"Marc's proposal was a shock to me too, Miss Wilkins," she said evasively. "But you know how intense a whirlwind romance can be. Almost before a man and woman know what's happening, they find themselves engaged. That's how it happened with us, isn't it, Marc *darling?"*

"Exactly, *amare mia,"* he agreed, smiling wickedly into her eyes and seemingly unaware of Brandi's deepening frown. Lowering his head, he allowed his lips to linger evocatively on Leigh's for a long moment before straightening again. "You might even say it was love at first sight."

Chapter Nine

Two days later, Angelica and Leigh sat at an umbrella-shaded table by the swimming pool watching Brandi Wilkins rise from the turquoise waters like an exquisite nymph ascending gracefully up the pool's tiled steps. A barely decent, black satiny bikini clung to her perfect body, accentuating, more than concealing, the generous fullness of her breasts. Ignoring her audience completely, she slipped a black satin ribbon from her hair and naturally platinum tresses tumbled down around her shoulders.

At the table, when Leigh sighed involuntarily, Angelica grimaced and tossed her hand in a dismissive gesture. "She is beautiful to look at but that is all. Signora Rossetti says it is more important for a person to be beautiful inside, too. And you are pretty inside and out."

A grateful smile tugged at the corners of Leigh's mouth but brought no accompanying sparkle to her eyes. "Still, I wouldn't mind being as beautiful as she is on the outside, too. It couldn't hurt."

"No, she is too tall," Angelica pronounced critically. "And her lips are too thin. You have a much prettier mouth than she does."

"Come on now, Angie, you have to admit she's one of those rare beauties who looks terrific, even after a dip in the pool. Look at her. Aphrodite herself rising from the sea couldn't have looked better than that."

"Hmmph, she is still too tall, and her lips are too thin," Angelica argued, eyeing the topic of discussion with unconcealed disdain. "And she is not very friendly. Since she has been here she has hardly spoken to us, even though Uncle Marcus is too busy working to spend time with her. I do not even understand why she stayed after he told her he was engaged to you."

"Maybe she didn't believe he could possibly be serious about marrying me."

"Oh but she seemed to. I have never seen anyone who looked as surprised as she did when you agreed with Uncle Marcus."

Shrugging, Leigh said wryly, "Then maybe she thought she could change his mind. She acts like a very persistent lady." And it was true. In two days Brandi Wilkins had demonstrated her ability to stick like glue, the ability that had undoubtedly propelled her to superstardom. Born Velma Mae Sink, she had beaten the odds and far surpassed the thousands of other girls, just as beautiful as she, who had come out of nowhere to make it big in Hollywood. Despite her nearly embarrassing lack of acting talent, she had persevered—as she was obviously intending to persevere where Marc was concerned. Actually, she seemed challenged by the fact that he was unwilling to fall at her feet and rejoice because she had finally left her husband, and Leigh could only suppose he had known very well she would react that way to his lie about their engagement.

"Say nothing more, *signorina,*" Angelica warned suddenly, interrupting Leigh's thoughts. "She is coming over to join us, I think. She must be getting very, very bored if she is willing to talk to us."

Ignoring the younger girl's sarcasm, Leigh lifted her head and smiled. "Did you have a nice swim, Miss Wilkins?"

"Scrumptious," Brandi purred, sitting down at the table and arranging her black fishnet beach jacket so that it accented her fair hair and darkly tanned body to best advantage. "But I really must start using a sunscreen, though I really don't want to. Despite my light hair I tan so easily. Why, I can get brown as a berry without even trying, but still, they do say the sun ages the skin and I wouldn't want that, no indeedy."

When Angelica silently mimicked Brandi's last words and wrinkled her nose in disgust as the woman looked away for a moment, Leigh fought to suppress a smile. "Would you care for something cool to drink, Miss Wilkins? I'd be glad to go in and ask Signora Rossetti to make some lemonade."

"Oh, I might have something a bit stronger than that in a few minutes, but right now I'd rather get to know you two," Brandi said, too sweetly. "I've just been so preoccupied the past few days that I haven't had a chance to talk to you. I do hope you understand I didn't mean to be rude, but I've been thinking about the television special I'll be filming next week and about a million and one other things that I have to do." Lounging back in her chair, she stretched one long lovely leg and admired the scarlet nail polish that graced the tips of perfectly pedicured toes. "I never realized how demanding the acting profession can be but—oh well, that's enough about me. Marc tells me you enjoy swimming, Angelica, so why didn't you come join me in the pool."

When the younger girl only shrugged, Leigh interceded teasingly. "Angelica only swims when Marc can.

I guess she just doesn't trust me to keep her from drowning."

"But that is not true! Not anymore, Leigh," Angelica assured her loyally. "I—I said that when you first came here, but now I know you are a very good swimmer. It is just more fun when Uncle Marcus swims with us. You think so too."

"I bet she does," Brandi commented, not quite able to mask the sarcasm in her voice as she turned her full attention to Leigh. "How long have you known Marc, Miss Sheridan? I can't recall ever hearing him mention you."

"Oh, we only met about four weeks ago," Leigh answered, twirling a button on the blue and white seersucker sundress she wore, "when I came here to be Angelica's companion."

"Angelica's companion?" Brandi exclaimed incredulously, sitting up straight in her chair. "But I thought you were just visiting him, that you were a guest here, like me. I had no idea you were an employee."

"She is not an employee anymore, *signora,*" Angelica spoke up resentfully, black eyes flashing. "She is now my uncle's fiancée."

"Yes, but I thought he had met you in some other way," Brandi told Leigh, a self-satisfied little smile beginning to curve her lips. "You mean you and he have only known each other a month and you're already making plans to get married? Rushing things a little, aren't you?"

"Oh, I don't know," Leigh answered vaguely. "As I said the other night, a whirlwind romance can really sweep you off your feet. Marc can be very persuasive—as I'm sure you realize, and he insisted we make plans right away."

"And I know why," Brandi muttered to herself, faking a smile and leaning forward to rest her arms on the table. "I think we should have a nice little chat—alone."

The hint was far from subtle and Angelica muttered begrudgingly, "I will go look for Camellia, then visit with Signora Rossetti in the kitchen for a while, Leigh, if you want to find me."

"We won't be long, dear," Brandi promised breezily, giving the girl a wink as she wheeled past in her chair. "You'll have your companion back in just a few minutes if you'll run along and play, uh, I mean, you can't *run* along of course, but if you'll go along and play—"

"I know what you mean, *signora,* and I am going," Angelica said, lifting her eyes heavenward in disgust as she rolled away.

"Oh dear, I hope I didn't hurt her feelings by saying that about running," Brandi whispered loudly to Leigh. "I simply didn't think."

I bet you rarely do, Leigh was tempted to retort. Instead she sat back in her chair and tried to relax, preparing herself for what she knew was going to be a grand inquisition.

"Well now, I think we should have a talk about Marc, don't you?" Brandi asked, forgetting completely about his niece. "Are you really in love with him?"

As she admitted it for the first time to herself, Leigh saw no point in lying. "Yes, I think I really am, but I suppose you think you are too."

Brandi sighed dreamily. "Oh my yes, and I've been in love with him a lot longer than you have. I've known Marc for years and years—well, it can't be that many years, because I'm only twenty-nine—but anyway, I've known him for a long time. Of course we were always attracted to each other, but nothing had ever come of it until this Spring when we ran into each other in Paris. Arthur—he's my husband—wasn't with me and—"

"Spare me the details, please," Leigh said dully. "Just make your point."

"Oh all right, if that's the way you want it I'll be brief," Brandi muttered disappointedly, drumming her fingers on the tabletop. "I think Marc has gotten himself engaged to you on the rebound because he was so upset with me. I mean, he actually just walked right out of my life when he realized I hadn't left Arthur! I tried to tell him it wasn't that easy for me to hurt poor Arty. I mean, after all, he gave me my first big break as an actress in this movie for television he made. So, I can't just walk up to him and say it's all over, now can I?"

"That's for you to decide," Leigh answered, thinking uncharitably that poor Arty would be much better off without a wife like her. But as she remembered that men obviously saw attributes in Brandi that she couldn't see, she smiled ruefully. "So you think Marc only proposed to me because he couldn't have you?"

"Exactly! Oh, I'm so glad you understand," the older woman bubbled insensitively. "The situation could have turned into something so unpleasant if you'd decided to try to hang onto him now that I'm free. You just don't know how grateful I am to you."

"Don't be grateful. I'm not about to break my engagement to Marc," Leigh said perversely, unwilling to allow Brandi to stop worrying yet. "If he decides he wants you, he'll have to break our engagement himself. Sorry."

"But—but he's so stubborn, he might not do that right away," Brandi said, an angry flush coloring her cheeks. "How can you let him use you that way? Doesn't it hurt your pride to know you want a man who doesn't really want you?"

"That's only your opinion," Leigh said calmly, rising to her feet. "Have you ever seriously considered the possibility that it might be *you* he doesn't want anymore?"

Brandi's laugh was an insult. "I certainly can't believe he wants you instead. Oh, you're pretty enough, I suppose, but my dear, you're just too young for a man like Marc. And obviously even he knows that. After all, he calls you his baby."

"But I happen to like him to call me his baby," Leigh said softly, a far away, reminiscent look in her eyes. "I like it very much." Pretending to rouse herself from some wonderfully evocative memory, she shook her head then shrugged nonchalantly. "Oh well, I guess we'll just have to wait and see what happens, won't we? Now if that's all you had to say to me, I think I'll go look for Angelica. See you later."

Brandi was muttering to herself and as Leigh walked away she smiled at her small victory—though her hands were trembling violently with delayed reaction to her bluff. Since Brandi Wilkins apparently considered herself God's gift to the world, it certainly wouldn't hurt her to be taken down a peg or two, at least temporarily. Yet giving Brandi something to fret about really didn't change Leigh's situation in the least. In this game she was destined to be the ultimate loser, and as she reminded herself of that fact, the thrill of her minor victory subsided and the deep depression she had been feeling since Saturday night settled in again. How was she ever going to be able to forget Marc, she wondered, sighing bleakly as she went through the open French doors to the salon. Before her eyes could adjust from the bright sunlight to the dimmer interior, she nearly stumbled over Angelica sitting in her chair in the center of the room.

"I was about to come for you, Leigh," the girl said, inclining her head toward the blue brocade sofa. "Brandi has a visitor waiting to see her—her husband."

"Husband," Leigh repeated weakly, her eyes darting to the man seated across the room who had immediately risen to his feet. Though he was at least thirty years his wife's senior, he was a fine-looking man, tall and slim with silvery streaked hair, and an unmistakable glint of determination in his eyes. As he nodded his head in a greeting to Leigh, she groaned inwardly. His arrival should cause quite a commotion. She forced herself to return his nod. "You're Mr. Wilkins?"

"No, I'm Arthur Preston, but I am Brandi's husband," he said with some amusement. "Brandi goes by her stage name, which causes occasional confusion." The explanation given, he waved his hand in Angelica's general direction. "This charming young lady let me in, but she doesn't seem to know where my wife is at the moment. But perhaps you could help me."

"Maybe I should get Mr. Cavalli," Leigh suggested hastily. "I—I'll go tell him you're here."

"He is in his darkroom," Angelica spoke up, her eyes wide with excitement. "I checked in his study when I was looking for Camellia and I saw the red light on."

"Do you know where my wife is, miss?" Arthur Preston asked rather impatiently. "If you do, I see no point in disturbing Marc at his work."

Before Leigh had to decide whether to lie or tell the truth, a startled gasp drew everyone's attention to the French doors where Brandi stood framed in the sunlight, her slender fingers pressed against her lips.

"Arty, wh—what a surprise," she uttered haltingly, with a weak fluttering of her other hand. "How—how did you know I was here?"

"Oh, I have my informants everywhere, didn't you know that, honey?" he replied quite pleasantly. "And since you're such a gadabout, I have to make use of them. Perhaps the next time you decide to take a trip you'll remember to tell me where you're going. You had me worried, leaving only days before we have to start taping your special. Actually, knowing what a scatterbrain you can be sometimes, I was afraid you'd forgotten all about it, so I decided I should fly over here and take you home."

Taking two steps into the room, Brandi shook her head obstinately. "But I'm not ready to go—"

"Art, it's been a long time," Marc suddenly interrupted, as he came into the room from the hall. Without showing one whit of concern, he strode toward the older man, holding out his hand in greeting. "What brings you to Capri?"

"My wandering wife, what else?" Arthur Preston said with an incredibly indulgent smile. "I was afraid she'd forgotten her television special she's to tape next week, so here I am to make sure we don't get sued for breach of contract."

As Leigh and Angelica exchanged stymied glances at the unexpectedly friendly conversation, Brandi regained her composure sufficiently to march across the room to stand before the two men, her hazel eyes ablaze with indignation.

"Would you two mind not talking about me as if I'm not even here?" she demanded crossly. "I'm perfectly capable of keeping up with my own schedule. I hadn't forgotten the taping next week, Arty, so you wasted your time coming here."

Gripping her upper arms lightly, Arthur pulled her to him and placed a kiss against her smooth forehead. "I don't feel it's wasted, honey. I thought we could spend a few days in Rome alone together, before we fly home."

"Rome certainly is exciting this time of year," Marc commented, almost as if he welcomed the other man's idea. "I can recommend it."

"But Marc!" Brandi gasped, reaching out for his arm then letting her hand drop when he discreetly, but deliberately, pulled away. "You—We—"

"We've enjoyed your stay with us," he said, his expression completely unreadable. "Maybe you can drop by again some time for a few days after Leigh and I are married."

"But Marc, you can't really mean to—"

"Come along honey, and I'll help you with your packing," Arthur said, guiding her toward the doorway to the hall. "I can't wait to get to Rome. Can you?"

When they were gone, Leigh's eyes sought Marc's face, catching a glimpse of pity for the older man in his eyes, but even as she recognized the emotion she couldn't really believe that was what she had seen. Surely he wasn't so noble that he was willing to give up Brandi simply because he felt sorry for her husband?

"I don't understand you," she whispered compulsively as he met her dumbfounded gaze. "I really don't understand you at all."

"I don't understand you either, but I'm about to change that," he answered crisply. "You're going to tell me exactly why you gave information about me to that Rome newspaper and you're going to tell me right now. Angelica, would you leave us alone for a few minutes?"

"Yes, Uncle Marcus," she agreed swiftly, turning her chair around, then halting abruptly when the phone on the corner desk began to ring. "D—do you want me to answer that for you?"

"I'll get it myself." After a look that told Leigh not to move from the spot where she was standing, he strode across the room to the phone.

"Do not be so scared, Leigh," Angelica whispered comfortingly. "Remember—what is it they say—his bite is not so bad as his bark."

"I wish I could believe that," Leigh muttered weakly, her pulse pounding sickeningly fast in her temples. Then as she watched Marc warily, she seemed to have been granted a reprieve as he hung up the phone. His angry expression had altered to one of concern and he didn't even look her way as he came back. Instead, he went to bend over Angelica's chair, brushing a loose strand of dark hair back from her thin face.

"I'm afraid I have disappointing news for you, *piccola,*" he said gently. "That was your mother and she said she won't be able to get back here when she promised, but she said tell you she will come as soon as she can."

"I knew she would not come back. I knew it!" Angelica cried, bursting into a storm of tears and spinning her chair around him and away toward the French doors.

"Let her be alone for a minute," Leigh suggested softly, tears of sympathy filling her eyes. "She's been talking about her mother coming back since the day she left, so it will take a little while for her to get used to having to wait a little longer."

"Damn Sophia! How could she do this to her?" Marc muttered furiously, then pressed his hand against Leigh's shoulder impelling her toward the doors. "Go after her. At least she can confide in you."

Leigh stepped onto the piazza a few seconds later, just in time to see the accident but not in time to prevent it. As Angelica sped across the tile surrounding the pool, Camellia leapt out from beneath a bordering shrub, playing friskily as usual. To avoid hitting her pet, Angelica turned too sharply. One wheel of her chair dropped over the edge of the pool and she was dumped in, headfirst. Calling for Marc over her shoulder, Leigh raced to the water's edge, kicking off her sandals because, though Angelica was usually an adequate swimmer despite her lifeless legs, she had panicked now and was thrashing about helplessly.

By the time Marc reached them, Leigh had already dived in and surfaced behind Angelica, clasping her arm across the girl's chest. Unfortunately, they were in the deepest end and it wasn't easy even to tread water with Angelica fighting every inch of the way.

"I have her now," Marc said finally, catching his niece under the arms and hauling her out to gather her close against him as he whispered, "Stop your crying, *piccola.* You're all right now. Everything's okay." And as Angelica's loud bawling became soft hiccoughing sobs, he looked over her head at Leigh. "How about you? Are you okay?"

"Wet, but fine," she said breathlessly, clinging to the

edge of the pool. "Why don't you take her up to her room and I'll be there as soon as I change clothes."

A half hour later, Leigh sat by Angelica's bed, towel-drying her own hair, watching impotently as the girl tossed her head restlessly on her pillow in her sleep. As Leigh leaned out to touch the thin hand laying on top of the bedcovers, Marc came back from calling the doctor, walking across the room on silent feet.

"Exhausted herself crying, didn't she?" he whispered, his gaze moving over Leigh with slow intensity. "Are you sure you're all right? No ill effects from the rescue?"

"Only stringy hair," she replied wryly, hoping to coax a smile from him. Instead he cupped his hand over her cheek, brushing his thumb against the delicate skin beneath her eyes.

"You're hair is beautiful. You're beautiful," he murmured, his eyes darkening to forest green. "You didn't have to do what you did, you know. She was fighting like hell and she could have easily drowned both herself and you."

"I knew you'd be there," Leigh said, then hesitated, glancing at Angelica. "But there's something you should know, Marc. When I was in the water with her, her legs moved."

"You're sure?" he exclaimed softly. "You're sure her legs didn't just drift against you?"

"No, she kicked me. Not very hard, of course, but she definitely kicked me."

"That is not true, Uncle Marcus!" Angelica cried suddenly, struggling to sit up in bed. "M—my legs did not move. I know they did not move. They will not move! Why are you saying that, Leigh? I thought you were my friend, but if you are going to lie about me, I do not want you in my room—so go away! Uncle Marcus, make her go away!"

As the girl began sobbing violently again, Leigh

shrank away from the bed, chewing her lower lip, having no idea what to say or do. Her wide, pain-darkened eyes met Marc's and to her dismay, filled with tears.

"She didn't mean what she said, Leigh," he comforted, taking her hand to help her up from the chair. "She's still half-hysterical but after the doctor gives her a sedative, she'll probably forget she ever said those things to you."

"I'm not so sure," Leigh whispered miserably. "Since it took her so long to start trusting me, I'm afraid she'll never be able to regain that faith again, now that she thinks I've lied about her. Oh, I wish I'd never mentioned her legs moving."

"Why? You weren't lying, were you?"

"Of course not but—"

"But nothing," he interrupted, silencing her with one finger against her lips. "You had to tell me and I'll have to tell the doctor. Even if she refuses to believe it, it has to be encouraging that in a moment of panic, her legs did move."

"Yes I know but—"

"You need to rest too," he said, leading her to the door. "Go lie down awhile and try to relax. Then when Angelica wakes up later, I'm sure she'll ask to see you."

Too weary to express any more doubts, Leigh obediently left the room, but as she stopped in the hall by her own door, she stared sadly back behind her for a brief moment. She wished she could share his confidence that Angelica would eventually forgive her, but unfortunately, she didn't believe he actually knew what a stubborn little girl his niece could be.

The air turned muggy and oppressive that night and Leigh tossed and turned in her bed. Though she pounded her pillow and switched positions countless times, she only succeeded in wadding up the bedclothes beneath her. She simply couldn't get comfortable. Finally she sat up straight, uttering an exasperated curse. All she needed to top off this rotten day was insomnia. The last thing she wanted to do was to lie awake and relive every disaster. Suddenly she wished she had never left the States. She certainly hadn't needed to come to Italy and get involved with a man who now thought she was a spy and with a girl who now considered her a traitor. She had allowed both Marc and Angelica to become far too important to her, and now she didn't know what to do to ease herself out of the situation without being badly hurt. How could she fall out of love with him, and how did she suppress the maternal feelings Angelica had awakened in her? It wouldn't be possible to simply walk away and forget them though she guessed that was what she would have to try to do. Believing her to be the source of that newspaper item, Marc certainly wouldn't want her around any longer, and since Angelica had refused all evening to even see her, it seemed as if her job here had ended anyway.

Maybe it would be best if she did just pack up and go home to the States, she rationalized, resting her forehead against her drawn up knees. After over four weeks here, Marc still remained an enigma, and his relationships with both Sophia and Brandi were beyond her unworldly comprehension. Yet her own relationship with him was even more confusing. Sometimes he could be so tender, while at other times, he acted as if he'd love to wring her neck, and now that he believed he had proof she was supplying information about him to newspapers, she could hardly expect to experience any more of his tenderness. Even if she told him the truth, that Stefano had obviously supplied the information, he would still blame her.

"Oh damn, damn, damn," she muttered, swinging

her feet to the floor, utterly weary of the same thoughts going round and round incessantly in her mind. Feeling as if the walls were closing in, she wandered barefoot onto the balcony, hoping for a breath of fresh air, but it was still and muggy, even outside. Most of the sky was overcast and only a cream-colored sliver of the moon shone dim light through the trees and danced with a faint sparkle on the surface of the water in the swimming pool. Suddenly, she longed to be in that water, and without a second thought, she went back inside to the adjoining bathroom to get her blue maillot swimsuit. Unfortunately, it was still damp from an early morning dip in the pool and she didn't relish the idea of having that clammy thing next to her skin. Undaunted, however, she went to ferret out from a dresser drawer the white, crocheted bikini she had bought only because her roommate had dared her to. She had never worn it anywhere—it had always seemed too shockingly brief—but she decided that wouldn't really matter tonight since she would be swimming alone in an unlighted pool. After putting it on she covered herself with her terry beach jacket, got a towel from the bathroom, then crept out of her room down the dimly lighted stairs.

The water felt as delightfully warm and silkily soft as she had imagined it would, and she breathed a contented sigh as she waded in up to her breasts. Pushing off the bottom with one foot, she floated lazily on her back in the center of the pool, completely relaxed as she gazed up at the moonlight flitting with eerie luminescence through the clouds overhead. Finally, she mustered the energy to turn and dive to the bottom, then allow herself to spiral slowly to the surface. Recalling manuevers from her old days in the water ballet, she glided across the surface, making only the smallest ripples as her arms and legs moved gracefully in perfect unison. At last her limbs rebelled and she rolled over onto her back again to rest. Everything was perfectly quiet. Not even the usually noisy cicadas were breaking the silence tonight. She closed her eyes, relaxing her body completely.

Without warning, her ankle was enclosed in a vise that tugged slightly, giving her time enough to instinctively take a breath before she was pulled beneath the surface completely by a fast, jerking motion. Before she had time to panic, her ankle was freed and two large hands spanned her waist while her own hands came to rest against a muscular, hair-roughened chest. It was Marc; she knew that even though she could only see a dark silhouette in the water before her. Relaxing again, she gripped his shoulders lightly as his strong kicks propelled them to the surface.

"You might have given me heart failure," she fussed weakly, after taking a deep breath. Still held by him, she tilted her head back to look into his shadowed face. "It wasn't very fair of you to scare me that way."

"But why should you be scared of being pulled underwater? From what I've just seen, you must be a mermaid," he said softly, brushing his fingers through her hair which trailed out behind her on the surface of the water. "I didn't know you were such an excellent swimmer. Why haven't you shown Angelica and me what you could do? I'm sure she'd love to see."

"I guess I've just been too busy watching you—helping Angelica with her exercises, I mean," Leigh added hastily as he impelled her back toward the shallow end of the pool where he could stand. Though her feet still didn't touch the bottom, she overcame the instinct to tread water. Marc's arm round her waist holding her lightly to him assured her she wasn't going to sink. Besides, there seemed to be far more to fear from the muscular body that was brushing against the barely-clad softness of her own. Deep water was no threat to her; she could always swim out of it but she knew Marc might not be so easy to escape, and more disturbing still, she knew she might not even want to escape him. Her fingers fluttered uncertainly on his chest. "Marc, I—"

Her words were halted by an initially gentle kiss that became, almost immediately, a passionate exploration. Twining his fingers in her hair, he pulled her head back slightly, forcing her to submit to the seeking hardness of his mouth—not that she needed to be forced. Her lips had parted breathlessly at the first touch of his and her mouth was opening, inviting the possessive, evocative invasion of the tip of his tongue. Yet, when his kisses burned in the hollow beneath her jaw, down her slender neck to the hollow between her breasts, she struggled to control her inflamed senses.

"No, no, I won't let you," she whispered urgently, pushing at his chest with her hands. "I won't let you use me as a substitute for Brandi, just because you felt sorry enough for her husband to let her go back to him."

"You little nitwit, who the hell do you think told Arty she was here?" Marc muttered harshly, gripping her hair and tugging it painfully. "I wanted him to come here and get her. I told you I can only contend with one woman at a time—and now that woman happens to be you."

Leigh's eyes widened, shining in the dim moonlight. "But Brandi said—"

"Brandi says a lot of things that aren't true. In Paris, she told me she'd left Arthur so I took her out a few times until the rumors about us started and I realized she hadn't left him at all. She was just having a fling, and I don't make it a practice of having flings with married women, so I left Paris and came here to get on with compiling my book."

Shaking her head, not quite convinced, Leigh gazed up at the shadowed, rugged contours of his face. "But that doesn't mean you don't still want her. She's very beautiful and you—"

"If ever I wanted her, meeting you changed my mind, don't you know that?" he whispered close to her ear. "Why can't I convince you that you're who I want now? Only you, Leigh. And I think I'll go crazy if I don't make love to you soon."

His words tumbled all the defenses she had built against him, and her response was guided by some inborn feminine instinct. Yielding eagerly to his superior strength, she slipped her arms up round his neck and pressed herself against him. Her legs entangled with his and when she felt the proof of his need for her against her thigh, she couldn't pull away. Instead, she moved seductively against him, smiling slightly as he groaned softly and crushed her to him. His mouth descended hungrily on hers and she explored the contours of his ears and the smooth column of his neck with trembling fingers, unable to think coherently, even as his fingers tugged at the strings of her top, tied behind her back and round her neck. The crocheted cups were replaced by the warmth of his hands curving round the firm fullness of her breasts. When he lifted her up in his arms, out of the water, and his lips closed over one taut tender nipple, her fingernails dug into the straining muscles of his shoulders.

"Oh Marc, yes," she breathed against his throat, moaning softly as his hand closed on her upper thigh and his fingers, brushing lightly against her, sent a burning shaft of pleasure blazing through her. Trembling with the hot desires he aroused, she clung to him, surrendering with a whispered, "I—I want you too."

"I'll make you forget your silly Stefano," he promised hoarsely. "Tonight you'll think of no one except me."

"I never think of anyone else when you touch me," she admitted, teasing his firm lower lip with gentle little bites as he carried her up the tiled steps, out of the pool to the circular, inflated float that lay on the concrete by the bordering myrtle tree. As he put her down gently and his body lowered to cover hers, she reached up to touch the creases beside his mouth, smiling up at him as his teeth closed on one fingertip. "I never think of anyone but you, ever."

"You're so beautiful," he murmured against her lips. "So warm and soft and beautiful. And I need you to give yourself completely to me."

"I want to," she whispered, urging his hand up from her waist to cover her bare, throbbing breast, trembling as his thumb brushed slowly back and forth over the hard, sensitized peak.

"*Bambina mia,* my baby who's not a baby at all," he muttered, then took her mouth roughly, with relentless demand, though his hands moving down to press against her hipbones conveyed an inexpressible gentleness.

Amazingly, she wasn't scared. Nothing mattered except pleasing him by giving him all her love, and her slender body was pliant beneath the hard, heavy weight of his. Even when he loosened one side-tie of her bikini and his fingers grazed her abdomen, she stiffened, then trembled violently, but made no effort to resist.

"Relax," he coaxed, his lips playing with the parted softness of hers. "Why are you shaking so? Surely you know you don't have any reason to be afraid of me, don't you?"

"Yes, I know. Oh, Marc, kiss me," she said breathlessly, a tremulous sigh signalling total submission.

Yet a moment later, as she burrowed her face against his neck while his hands sent shivers of excitement coursing through her, everywhere he touched, she moaned softly. But there was an involuntary hint of appeal in her voice as she whispered his name.

He lifted his head, gazing down at her with passion-brightened eyes. "You're scared and you shouldn't be," he whispered, brushing a strand of damp hair from her cheek. "I'm going to be very gentle with you, so try to relax. You're trembling as if no man has ever touched you this way before and I know—." His words halted as she averted her eyes shyly, evoking from him a sharp intake of breath. Then he was moving away abruptly, rolling over onto his back beside her, stilling her hand as it brushed tentatively across his chest.

"Marc, what is it?" she asked bewilderedly. "Did—did I do something wrong?"

"Wrong?" he muttered huskily. "For God's sake, Leigh, you're a virgin! Aren't you?"

"Yes, but—"

"But *I didn't know that!*" he exclaimed roughly. "Now I realize I probably should have guessed, but that damned picture I took of you and your boyfriend, plus that little episode in Rome, convinced me he was your lover." Reaching over to her he feathered his fingers across her cheek then tensed as she drew his hand back down to cover her breast. "Leigh, don't! You can't begin to know how much I still want you."

"Then make love to me, Marc. It doesn't matter that I've never—"

"It matters to me!" he groaned, jerking his hand away to sit up, his back to her. "I don't especially want you to hate me in the morning."

"But I wouldn't," she murmured, trailing one finger down his spine. "I could never hate you."

"Leigh, don't tempt me," he commanded hoarsely. "I don't expect you to pay for spying on me with your virginity."

His words were like ice cold water thrown in her face and her breath caught deep in her throat.

"Wh—what are you saying? You mean this was supposed to be a punishment for me because you think I spied on you?" she whispered, her voice choked.

"That's all this was? Oh my God, you *can* be ruthless, can't you?"

"Leigh, I didn't mean that the way it sounded. Leigh!" he called, but before he could catch her hand she was on her feet, grabbing her beach jacket, then running, stumblingly back toward the house.

Chapter Ten

Leigh was up relatively early the next morning, and despite the fact that she had only slept a couple of hours she was amazingly clear-headed, too clear-headed, actually, for her peace of mind. She would have preferred the events of last night to have become fuzzy memories, but instead she could recall every humiliating moment in quite vivid detail. Though her head ached abominably, she even had the presence of mind to remember that she had left the top of her swimsuit somewhere around the pool. Dressing hastily in a denim skirt and knit top, she slipped her feet into cork-soled espadrilles and ran downstairs and out onto the piazza, hoping she could save herself more humiliation by finding the bra before someone else did.

It was nowhere to be found, though she searched everywhere. It wasn't floating embarrassingly in the pool, nor was it anywhere on the surrounding deck. After circling the pool several times, she stood morosely by the spot where she was certain Marc had taken it off her. It was obvious someone else had found it and she felt an odd urge to laugh and cry at the same time as she realized what that person must be thinking of her right now. All she could hope was that Angelica wasn't that person. She was confused enough without having to wonder what kind of relationship her uncle was having with a companion she no longer trusted.

Her head bent, hands stuffed into the pockets of her skirt, Leigh walked slowly back to the house, but as she stepped through the doorway into the salon, she froze suddenly as Marc stepped forward—seemingly out of nowhere—to block the way.

"Looking for something out there?" he asked very softly.

Though her cheeks flamed, she met his eyes directly. "My—uh—oh, you know exactly what I was looking for."

"Yes, and I have it in my room," he replied calmly, catching her wrist as she tried to flounce past him. "You can get it later, but right now I think we should discuss what happened last night."

"There's nothing to discuss," she said stiffly, tugging her arm, trying to free herself. "I got your message loud and clear."

"For God's sake, Leigh, listen to me," he muttered, his hands descending on her shoulders to lightly massage the tensed muscles beneath his fingers. There was something oddly urgent in the expression on his tan face. "I want to explain—"

He was interrupted by a clatter of footsteps on the marble floor in the main gallery, and a puzzled frown creased his brow as the doors to the salon opened.

"Sophia—I didn't expect you after your phone call yesterday," he said, releasing Leigh's shoulders only to catch her hand in his so she couldn't walk away. "What made you change your mind about coming? It must have been important to get you out of bed this early in the day."

His sister-in-law, looking far less *soignée* than usual, smiled weakly and smoothed the skirt of her rather rumpled, blue linen suit. "It—it is important. I am just beginning to see how important. After I talked to you yesterday and you were so harsh with me for not coming back to see Angelica, I realized what a terrible mother I was being—what a terrible mother I have always been. But I am going to try to do better. It does no good to run away from responsibilities. I have not even been very happy all these years when I allowed other people to take care of her for me. She is my daughter and I will start treating her that way—if she will let me now. Do—do you think she can ever forgive me for disappointing her the way I did yesterday?"

"Oh, I think so," Marc said gently. "And you couldn't have picked a better time to realize you love her. I imagine she needs you more today than she has ever needed you before." He went on to explain about Angelica's spill in the pool and the deep depression that had followed, concluding, "Yes, I think she'll be glad to forgive you."

Sophia twisted her hands together nervously in front of her. "C—could I see her now? Is she awake?"

"I'll get her for you, Signora Cavalli," Leigh offered, feeling an odd mixture of relief and disappointment as Marc released her hand. Then, as she passed the older woman on the way out, she tried to smile encouragingly. "I'm glad you came back, *signora.* Maybe Angelica will forgive me too, since I'll be giving her the good news that you're here."

Leaving Marc to explain his niece's resentment toward her, Leigh ran lightly up the stairs, down the hall to Angelica's room. She tapped once on the door, then went in, sighing inwardly as she saw that the girl was still in bed, though she was awake and staring at the ceiling.

"I have something very exciting to tell you," she announced as she approached the bed. "Why don't you get up and I'll help you dress while I tell you what it is."

"Wait, Leigh," the girl muttered, struggling up to support herself on her elbows, her eyes dark with unhappiness. "I am sorry I was so mean to you yesterday. I know that you really believe my legs moved because you like me and you want me to be able to walk. It was ugly of me to say you were lying when you were really only mistaken. I am very sorry. Will you still be my friend?"

"Nobody could stop me," Leigh said huskily, bending down to give the girl a brief hug. Then she straightened with a tremulous smile. "And I hope we can always be friends, even though you won't really need me anymore now. That's what I came to tell you—your mother is downstairs and she wants very much to see you, to apologize for upsetting you yesterday."

"Then I suppose she will go away again," Angelica said bitterly. "She did not have to come just to say she is sorry. I do not need her anyway."

"Yes you do, and she needs you too, very much," Leigh insisted, helping Angelica move from the edge of the bed into her chair. "I think you should give her another chance to be a mother to you. She seems ready to really try this time because, as she said, she hasn't been very happy all these years without you."

"She said that?" Angelica exclaimed, her eyes brightening. "Really? She has not been happy without *me?*"

"That's what she said."

"Then hurry, please. Bring me a dress to wear," the girl bubbled excitedly. "I do not want to keep her waiting for me or she might change her mind."

Five minutes later, as Leigh pushed Angelica's chair through the doorway to the salon, Sophia's back was turned and she was staring at Marc as he hung up the phone on the desk. Leigh stopped suddenly, sensing a nearly tangible tension in the air. When Marc turned to face all of them, the ashen tinge of his dark skin set her heart pounding.

"What is it, Marc?" Sophia asked squeakily. "What is wrong?"

"You'd better sit down, Sophia," he said grimly, hurrying to put his arm around her waist, taking a deep breath when she refused to let him lead her to the sofa. "All right. It's Roberto. He crashed his car during a rally near San Remo and—"

"*Papa!* He is dead!" Angelica cried out before he could finish.

At those words, total chaos ensued. Sophia uttered a tortured groan, and as she fainted and Marc scooped her up in his arms to put her on the sofa, Angelica rose to her feet, taking one unsteady step toward her mother before muscles, unused for over a year, rebelled and her legs crumpled beneath her.

Though astounded by the sight of Angelica standing, Leigh had quick enough reflexes to catch her and pull her back into the chair before she could fall. Marc dragged his surprised gaze from his niece back to Sophia whose eyes were beginning to flicker open.

"Mama, Mama, are you all right?" Angelica cried, wheeling her chair swiftly across the room to the sofa. "Uncle Marcus, is she all right?"

"I am all right, *bambina mia,*" Sophia answered for herself weakly, reaching out to drop a limp hand onto her daughter's knee. "I fainted very easily when I was pregnant with you too." As Angelica shook her head bewilderedly, Sophia gave a warm smile. "I did not mean to tell you in this way but—but now I must. You will have a brother or sister in a few months, *bambina.* I am expecting a baby."

At Marc's sharp intake of breath, Leigh's eyes darted to his face and the bottom seemed to drop out of her stomach at his dismayed expression. Did he fear it was his child his sister-in-law was expecting?

Sophia, too, noticed his reaction, and as she sat up slowly her lips trembled as she obviously fought against giving in to the tears gathering in her eyes. "Do not look so shocked, Marc darling," she said shakily. "It is Roberto's baby. We—we spent a week together in Cannes two months ago. There is still that attraction between us, and every time we meet it is the same. We spend a few days together, thinking we can make our marriage work, but then we start bickering like two small children and decide to go our separate ways again." As she shook her head sadly, a sob escaped her. "It is so crazy. In all these years, there has been no other man for me. I—I know Roberto has had his affairs but I—I guess I never stopped loving him. And now—now he is—"

"He isn't dead," Marc interrupted hastily. "Angelica didn't let me finish. He is badly hurt but he's alive. He's been flown to a hospital in Rome."

"I must go to him then!" Sophia jumped to her feet, pressing her hand against her forehead as she swayed slightly, but as Marc offered his arm to lean on, she shook her head. "I will be all right. Angelica will go with me to the bathroom and after I splash a little cold water on my face, I will not feel so lightheaded and we can leave for Rome."

"Will you tell him about the baby, Mama?" Angelica asked eagerly as she preceded her mother from the room. "Or will you wait?"

"Oh, I will tell him right away," Sophia said softly. "I could not keep such a secret from him. I will not wait a minute to tell him we are having a baby."

Then they were out in the hall and only Leigh heard Marc bleakly, "I just hope it's not already too late."

Leigh and Marc took the last ferry back to Capri from Naples late that night. Alone in the Mercedes, they talked very little and Leigh leaned her head wearily against the passenger window, watching the dark shapes of the trees swaying in the wind as the road wound upward toward the villa. Roberto was out of danger. Despite several broken ribs, a punctured lung, and a broken arm and leg, he had been conscious when they had all arrived at the Rome hospital. After a great flood of tears from Angelica and Sophia and he had overcome his shock about the coming baby, he and his wife had seemed to come to a tentative understanding. Angelica had promised her parents that she would try very hard to walk again if they would try as hard to make their marriage work, and when Marc and Leigh had left the hospital room Leigh felt very optimistic about Angelica's chances of finally having two parents who loved her.

Now, however, as they approached the drive to the villa, all optimism in general had drained away. She was tired and Marc's hurtful reluctance to talk on the drive from Rome had made her even more weary, especially after she had realized she had so little time left to be with him. With Angelica gone there was no reason for her to stay at the villa, and she was certain he would expect her to leave soon, probably tomorrow.

"Why is the house so dark?" she asked dully a moment later as they turned onto the private drive. "Signora Rossetti never turns out all the lights."

"Damn, I'd forgotten they both went into Naples early this morning," he muttered rather irritably. "Their daughter had a new baby so they'll be away for a couple of days taking care of two other grandchildren. I guess we'll have to fend for ourselves, won't we? Can you cook?"

"Fairly well," she murmured, her heart beginning to beat a little faster at the thought of being alone with him. "Why? Are you hungry?"

"God, no. Right now, I'm just exhausted."

Several minutes later as he unlocked the front door, switching on the lights that illuminated the main gallery and the upstairs hall, Leigh walked past him to stand uncertainly by the staircase. It seemed necessary to break the silence somehow and she asked rather lamely, "Do you think Roberto and Sophia will really get back together? After all that's happened, can they make their marriage work?"

"Sure, if they both decide to grow up before Angelica does, rather than with her," he answered with brutal but realistic candor. Shrugging, he raked his fingers through his hair. "Frankly, I can't worry about them at the moment, I'm too tired. And I know you must be too. I suggest we should get some sleep and hope tomorrow is a hell of a lot quieter than today has been."

A half-hour later, Leigh realized just how right he had been when she awakened with a start and saw that she had drifted off to sleep while soaking in the bathtub. Rising out of the now tepid water, she haphazardly dried herself with a towel, pulled her nightgown on and stumbled to her bed, falling asleep again almost before her head touched her pillow.

It was a dreadful wailing that awakened her again hours later, and she rubbed her eyes and sat up reluctantly in bed. As a flash of lightning brightened her room, followed by a loud rumble of thunder, the wailing became louder and it was then she realized she was hearing a very unhappy cat. Camellia, no doubt, believed she had been abandoned by everyone. Leigh could imagine the poor little thing, cowering at the kitchen door, begging to be let inside, where she could escape the coming storm.

Without stopping for slippers or robe, Leigh hurried downstairs, but she didn't find Camellia at the kitchen door as she had expected to. Actually, she didn't see the cat anywhere, even with the frequent flashes of lightning, but she could still hear that plaintive wailing. Rather reluctantly, she stepped outside and by following the sound, finally located the cat crouching just out of reach on a limb of a carob tree in the garden.

"You silly animal," she fussed as she began to climb the tree. "Why did you come up here if you're too much of a chicken to go back down?" Wrapping one arm around the branch to secure her position, she reached out for Camellia but just at that inopportune moment, lightning flashed and thunder popped loudly. The kitten spat and raked out with sharp claws. As Leigh cried out softly in pain, it scurried to the far end of the branch to cling precariously to a cluster of leaves as the limb swayed.

Muttering to herself, Leigh touched light fingertips to her undeserved wound, then nearly fell out of the tree from fright as Marc spoke from directly below her.

"What the hell are you doing up a tree in the middle of a thunderstorm?" he asked sharply. "Trying to get yourself struck by lightning?"

"It's Camellia," she explained, pointing to the cat at the end of the limb. "She's stuck up here."

"Not anymore." Marc reached up, grasped the cat by the scruff of her neck, and lowered her to safety. "Now, you're the only one stuck up there." Unceremoniously, he gripped Leigh's waist and lowered her down too, but not to the ground. Instead he kept her in his arms, close against him, shaking his head. "Don't you ever wear shoes if you don't have to?"

"You can't climb trees with shoes on," she muttered weakly. Then as her fingertips explored the stinging scratch on the gentle swell of her right breast, she complained, "That little monster scratched me! I was trying to rescue her and she scratched me."

"We'll put something on it when we get upstairs," he answered, controlling his amusement only with a great deal of effort. Yet he wasn't smiling when he returned to her room a few minutes later after leaving her to go get a bottle of antiseptic. "Here," he said flatly, "put some of this on the scratch and it should be all right."

Leigh lowered the right strap of her gown, partially exposing the gentle curve of her breast. "It'll sting," she murmured compulsively, lifting her eyes to him. "I don't think I can put it on there myself. W—would you do it for me?"

"I don't think I'd better," he muttered, turning on one heel and striding to the door. "Goodnight, Leigh."

Tears filled her eyes as she heard his footsteps recede down the hall. As she swabbed the antiseptic carelessly on her breast the stinging it caused became the final straw. She had been scratched by a cat and rejected for the second night running by the man she loved. It was too much. As she fell into bed, the tears started flowing silently and it wasn't until her pillow was soaked that she fell asleep again.

Leigh packed her belongings early the next morning, preparing for the inevitable. Obviously, whatever Marc had felt for her briefly had not been able to survive the doubts he had about her trustworthiness, so she had decided to tell him she was leaving before he could ask her to. Wanting to look her best when she saw him, she put on her white gauze sundress, and after brushing her hair and applying a hint of blusher to her unusually pale cheeks, she took a deep tremulous breath and left her room.

As she walked down the curving stairs, she told

herself again that she would show absolutely no emotion when she spoke to Marc. To allow him to see how much she loved him and how much she was hurt at the thought of leaving would only embarrass him and humiliate her. So she would be as cold-hearted and unresponsive as he had been the past two nights because that was the only way she could leave Villa Bianca with any of her pride intact. Lifting her chin determinedly, she squared her shoulders, but at the sound of angry voices coming from the salon, she halted abruptly near the foot of the stairs.

"I suppose you know I could call the police and have you arrested for trespassing," Marc was saying. "And I will if you don't tell me why you're here, photographer in tow, creeping around over the grounds. Just what were you trying to do?"

In the tense silence that followed, Leigh tiptoed down the last two steps, a perplexed frown knitting her brow. When Marc's question was answered, her face drained of all color as she recognized Stefano's voice.

"I heard that Brandi Wilkins was staying here," he said glibly. "And you know there is always a story wherever the incomparable Brandi is."

"You heard wrong though—Miss Wilkins is not here," Marc said tersely. "But I would still like to know where you heard that she was."

"Oh, around," Stefano answered evasively. "You know."

"Around Leigh Sheridan by any chance? I know she knows you. Did she tell you Brandi was here?"

Out in the hall, Leigh tensed, waiting to hear Stefano absolve her of all blame but, to her astonishment, he didn't.

After clearing his throat rather nervously, he made her sound like a despicable little schemer. "Ah, you know Leigh is a reporter then? I wondered how long she could keep you from finding that out."

Suppressing a violent urge to run in and rake her fingernails across Stefano's face, Leigh ran out the front door, unable to listen to any more damning half truths about herself. Her heart was thudding sickeningly as she searched for some place to hide until Marc's temper had a chance to cool. When she noticed a patch of red between the trees that bordered the curving drive, she started running again, stopping to catch her breath only when she reached Stefano's Ferrari.

The key was in the ignition and she got in, started the engine, and backed down the drive to the main road, feeling some grim satisfaction in using Stefano's own precious car to escape retribution for his lies.

The drive toward Capri wasn't exactly smooth. It had been several years since she had driven her older brother's sports car but, at the moment, she didn't care at all if she stripped every gear in Stefano's bright red status symbol. In fact, she thought she might enjoy doing just that. If anyone deserved vengeance wreaked upon him, that idiot did.

Too angry to really care where she went, she drove through Capri, down to Marina Grande where she got lucky for the first time in several days. The ferry to Naples was about to depart and she knew taking it was her best chance of escaping Marc's wrath for a few hours at least.

She parked the Ferrari carelessly, jumped out to run down to the quay, and was aboard the ferry with plenty of time to spare. Ignoring the admiring glances of a few members of the crew, she hurried to the far end to stand, her hands clutching the railing, as she tried to slow her heartbeat to normal. "What an insane mess," she muttered to herself as she stared down into the dark blue waters. Before, her life had always been so quiet and predictable, but since coming to Italy, everything had gone out of control and she wasn't sure she would ever be able to get back to normal again. Certainly, she wouldn't ever forget Marc, or the emotions he could evoke in her. It was devastating to realize she might never love any other man so completely. It was grimly amusing in a way. Cool, unresponsive Leigh had finally met a man who could seduce her without much effort and he didn't want her. He certainly felt no love for her, especially now, after Stefano's disgusting performance. "Oh damn," she whispered bleakly then uttered a little cry of fear as a tan hand suddenly encircled her wrist in a vise-like grip.

"Penny for your thoughts," Marc said, his voice deceptively calm as he herded her toward the boarding ramp at the other end of the ferry.

Leigh could hardly breathe, and her pulses were pounding with dizzying rapidity as she glanced sideways at the grim line of Marc's mouth. "Please listen," she whispered. "It isn't like Stefano made it sound. Can't you let me go to Naples for a few hours until you're not so angry? Then I'll come back and we can talk."

"We'll talk now. You have a lot of explaining to do."

Though she groaned inwardly at the fury conveyed by his clipped words, she balked stubbornly when he began threading through a group of women blocking the boarding ramp. As she resisted, Marc stopped among the women, turning around to her, a warning glimmer in his green eyes. "Move, Leigh, or I swear I'll throw you over my shoulder and carry you off."

Leigh moved, but her cheeks burned hotly as one of the women said something to Marc in Italian; all the women laughed when he answered with a grin. "What did you say about me to them?" she asked resentfully. "Why did they all laugh?"

Marc shrugged. "I only told them you were my very nervous bride of one hour."

"Ooh, you just love to humiliate me, don't you?" she exclaimed softly, glaring up at him as he coerced her into the passenger seat of his car, then came round to slide in behind the wheel.

"We'll talk about what I'd like to do to you when we get back to the villa," he announced flatly, driving away from the quay. "So just be quiet until we get there."

"Where is that idiot Stefano?" she disobeyed immediately. "If he's still at the villa, he may be very sorry. I could—could—"

"He rode down with me. By now, he's retrieved his stolen car and is probably on his way to Naples on the ferry."

"But—"

"Enough. I told you we'll talk when we get home, Leigh."

Pressing herself against the door, she felt her defensive anger dissolve. Only dread remained, a dread that increased considerably a few minutes later when they arrived at the villa.

Ominously silent, Marc marched her inside, into the salon, where he released her wrist to stand towering over her, feet wide apart, his hands thrust deep into his pockets. "Begin, Leigh," he commanded, his eyes cold and hard. "You tell me exactly why you came here and this time I want the truth."

Her story came out haltingly, beginning with her brief stint as a reporter in San Francisco and concluding with her becoming Angelica's companion because the job Stefano had promised never materialized.

"So you do admit that you're a reporter?" Marc said after she had finished. "Do you also admit being the source of those items about me in Marvini's gossip sheets?"

"No! I wasn't! Really. I came here to be a companion and that's all I ever was—honestly."

"And you deny telling Marvini Brandi was here?"

Leigh's chin quivered. "Oh Marc, how can you think I'd do that? I—I care about you—I'd never—"

"Do you care about me?" he whispered, taking both her hands and drawing her closer. "Is that why you would have let me make love to you the other night—when you've never let any man make love to you before? How much does that mean you care, Leigh?"

"I never gave anyone any information about you," she evaded the question nervously. "You have to believe me."

"Oh, I believe you," he said, smiling down at her. "Stefano finally admitted you weren't responsible for those newspaper items."

Her wide eyes darkened accusingly. "Then why are you so angry? Why did you—"

"Tell me how much you care, Leigh," he coaxed, brushing firm lips across her cheek. "If it's not enough, then I'll let you go, if that's really what you want to do."

As his hands sought her waist, she shook her head in utter confusion. "Why does it matter how much I care?" she asked, her voice a breathless whisper as he pulled her roughly against the hard length of his body. "Why?"

"Because," he murmured into her ear, "I think it would be very nice if you loved me, since I love you."

"*Marc?*" she breathed, her knees weakening. "D—do you? Really?"

"I love you like hell, you stubborn, rebellious, delicious little baby. How could I not? You're everything I want you to be: loving, intelligent, and a very sexy little wench," he said between light, teasing kisses along her jaw. "And you do love me too, don't you?"

"Oh, Marc, you know I do! I love you so much," she admitted, wrapping her arms tightly round his neck, laughing tearfully as he lifted her off her feet, crushing her to him. Yet, when he sat down on the sofa holding her on his lap, the laughter soon became urgent, whispered endearments between the intense, lingering kisses and intimate caresses they exchanged.

"I want you, Leigh," he said roughly, his breath warm in the scented hollow between her breasts. "I love you and I need you to belong to me."

Pulling away slightly, she traced the firm, sensuous outline of his mouth with one fingertip. "The other night by the pool," she began uncertainly, "why—why did you say that about making me pay for spying on you?"

"Leigh, I had to say something to make you stop touching me," he explained, his eyes loving as they swept slowly over her. "I wanted you so much—but I knew I'd hate myself if I let your first time happen on a plastic float by a swimming pool. I want to make our first time something very special, not something hurried and almost illicit. I want you to marry me. I want to make love to you slowly, all night long in a bed, in a cool, quiet room."

Smiling, she snuggled close to him. "I have a bed upstairs in a cool, quiet room," she whispered invitingly. "It isn't night but—"

"Leigh, are you sure you're ready?" he asked, his voice appealingly husky. "We can get married in three days, and if you want to wait until our wedding night, then I guess I can stand it."

"I love you, Marc," was her answer. "And I want to belong to you now."

"And I love you," he groaned, taking her mouth savagely, his hands cupping her breasts. Then he held her from him for a moment. "Does this mean you're finally willing to take off your clothes for me?"

Her cheeks colored attractively, and she felt suddenly shy as her gaze was captured and held by the passionate glimmer of his. "Well, I'm not sure I could just take them off myself but I think I would like it very much if you took them off for me."

"Hmmm, I think I'd like that too," he whispered against her parted lips. And lowering the back zipper of her dress, he began. A few minutes later, as he carried her up the stairs, his lips grazed the gentle curve of her breast above her bra and when she trembled, he shook his head. "Don't be afraid of me. Remember I love you, *bambina mia.*"

"You won't be able to call me that when we really have a baby," she murmured. "Will you?"

"We'll think about that much, much later," he answered with a wicked smile. "I think I'm going to want you to myself for quite some time to come. Okay with you?"

"Okay," was all she was allowed to say before his mouth was hard and seeking on hers. As he carried her into her room there was no longer any need for words, anyway.